When Your
Number's Up!

ORLA
KELLY
PUBLISHING

Patrick Osborne

Orla Kelly Publishing
27 Kilbrody,
Mount Oval,
Rochestown,
Cork,
Ireland.

Printed and bound in Ireland by www.printmybook.com

Dedication

To my wife, Liz for your unwavering support and unbelievable patience. To my three children Robert, David & Rebecca (my chief proofreader whose honest opinions I value).

To my Mam for encouraging me to write and to my Dad for his tall tales.

Praise for Patrick Osborne

"The characters and situations are very funny..." – Declan Lowney (Bafta winning director, Father Ted, Little Britain, Ted Lasso, Moone Boy).

"...Osborne has managed to capture the typical working-class Dub sense of humour with considerable finesse." – Anne Cunningham, Meath Chronicle.

"...it will appeal to fans of Roddy Doyle's Barrytown Trilogy..." – Garreth Murray, Irish Independent.

Acknowledgements

A big thank you to my wonderful publisher, Orla Kelly.

To everyone who has helped me along this writing journey, I couldn't have done it without you.

I'd also like to thank the Irish Writers' Centre for their support and to playwright, Colin Murphy for his excellent mentoring.

Last but not least, I'm extremely grateful to the Book Punk readers who know a thing or two about novels and who have given me great encouragement.

Chapter 1

"If it's meant for you, it won't pass you by!"

Dublin 1985.

Mrs. Bridges was short and plump with a pleasant, moon-shaped face which kind of suited her inner hippy. She was dressed in a tan coloured, corduroy skirt with matching jacket that was once all the rage when her life was more carefree. She gripped Patrick, her nine year old son's hand and led him up the sandstone steps of the imposing structure built sometime in the early nineteenth century. If local myth was to be believed the building was constructed on the wrong continent entirely after plans had been mixed up while the country was under British rule and that somewhere in India there were people being treated in an 'Irish' hospital or at least camped out in a packed Accident & Emergency room. A rectangular brass plaque in serious need of a bit of spit and polish was fixed to the wall with Oncology Department just about visible through the grime and dirt. 'Hopefully it wasn't a reflection of the standard of care being administered inside,' Mrs. Bridges thought to herself.

As soon as Mrs. Bridges and her son had pushed their way through the heavy wooden entrance doors they stiffened at the enormity of the lobby but were almost immediately bundled to one side by a disgruntled visitor hurrying past.

Mrs. Bridges gave the middle-aged man the benefit of the doubt and said nothing. 'You never knew what worries other people might have, especially when visiting sick people,' she thought. She always made allowances like that, something which used to drive her husband completely bonkers, not that he was in the least bit aggressive. Patrick removed his cumbersome, square-shaped glasses, courtesy of the health board, which had fogged up. He took the scrunched up piece of unused tissue from under the cuff of his jumper and wiped the lenses clear. He then stuck his glasses back on again, shoving them into place with his index finger. Although the lenses were scraped to bits he still had another four months to wait until he was entitled to another free pair. His mother was always going on at him not to be leaving them lying face down whenever he took them off but of course he never listened. He huddled in closer to her as they looked about in dreaded awe.

"I don't want to be here," he whispered.

"I know exactly how you feel," his mother answered, giving a little giggle in the hope that she was somehow fooling her only son.

The doctor sat across the darkly timbered desk from the concerned woman, wrestling his thumbs like two naked Olympians from ancient Greece engaged in mortal combat.

"There's this revolutionary new treatment in the United States, it's expensive…" the doctor began.

Mrs. Bridges shook her head unable to disguise her disappointment and resigning herself to her fate. Sensing this, the doctor gave a short, polite cough, not that he had to but it had become a habit of late when delivering bad news.

"Realistically, you're looking at two to three months, six at the very most I'm afraid," he bluntly revealed.

Mrs. Bridges looked forlornly out through the glass panelled wall at her son. He was sitting cross-legged on the hardwearing brown carpet which was flecked with grey as if a painter had shaken his wet brush all over it. It wasn't the most comfortable of surfaces but Patrick took no notice. He was well used to a lot less luxury and besides, he was far too busy playing with coloured wooden blocks, attempting to push one through a circular hole in a laminated board. It wouldn't fit but instead of giving up he turned the block around and tried again and again and again. Close by, another young lad was figuring out a complex jigsaw puzzle of an ocean scene with the gleaming white sail of a small boat in the distance. He turned his head towards a well dressed woman in her late thirties who was sitting bolt upright, casually flicking through a glossy magazine. She was unable to hide her smugness while secretly observing Patrick's pathetic struggle with the simple blocks. She beckoned for her son to come join her, fearing that the other boy's 'condition' might somehow be contagious. He obediently did as he was instructed, smirking and giving her what he believed to be a discreet and conspiratorial nod. Mrs. Bridges couldn't help but notice the silent exchange and though she had witnessed similar incidents in the past it still cut to the bone. She turned back to the doctor.

"What am I supposed to do with my boy?" she asked.

"Are there any other family members perhaps?" said the doctor.

"There's no one else," she regretfully answered, having longed for a large family but complications during Patrick's birth had put paid to that. She was in no doubt that had she been a private patient a lot more would have been done to help other than the botched job that subsequently led to an emergency hysterectomy. Her late husband was adamant at first that they should sue but after talking things through she'd convinced him that it wasn't the fault of the harassed nurses and that it wouldn't be right to destroy the career of the poor junior doctor who looked as if he hadn't slept in a week. They agreed that the system was broken and just thanked God that both mother and son had survived. They had also chatted at length about the possibility of fostering and although they both thought it would be a wonderful thing to do they were point blankly refused due to their financial standing and not quite living in the right area. Patrick had asked on numerous occasions about getting a little brother or sister and he would cross his heart and promise to help out except with the nappy changing duties of course. His parents had loved and enjoyed his innocence even though it pained them enormously to only have the one child. They would remind him time and again that he was their special gift and part of some bigger plan.

The medic cleared his throat, politely attempting to regain his patient's attention.

"The state has homes…" he began but was immediately shot down.

"Over my dead body," Mrs. Bridges angrily replied, "I've heard the stories as I'm sure you have too. Besides, he's not like other boys his own age."

She looked back out through the glass panels. Patrick was now jumping up and down, dancing on the coloured block of timber until it was tightly wedged in the circular hole. The smug woman was cowering in a corner, shielding her son who was crying hysterically. Patrick then lifted the board high above his head and began to smash it against the wall.

"He's very determined…" Mrs. Bridges added, her voice trailing off.

Although the earlier rain had cleared, a dark and ominous blanket of cloud still hung over Mrs. Bridges and her young son as they negotiated their way through the torrent of shoppers coming from Henry Street and onto Mary Street. Mrs. Bridges wouldn't normally have taken this route, instead using the numerous side streets and cobbled lanes she'd grown up in to avoid the chaos but she badly needed to get to the hardware shop. A shout of 'Sketch', the universal warning call for so many generations of Dubliners, was left out by a high pitched voice. The shoppers, like Meerkats on some dusty African plain, seemed to instinctively pause as one and cock their heads, checking for danger. Out of nowhere a convoy of street traders wearing headscarves and fur-lined ankle boots came charging towards Patrick and his mother, pushing prams laden with bunches of bananas and punnets of strawberries resting on bread boards. A number of the dealers also had contraband such as tobacco and fireworks hidden underneath or stashed down their modified petticoats. This was a time when money was tight and everyone was trying to make an extra few shillings just to keep food on the table. A boy in Patrick's class had told him that his mother and hundreds of women from the inner-city travelled to Lourdes every year coming up to the Halloween. And after they'd said their prayers, hoping for miracles, they'd stuff their suitcases with selection boxes full of Roman candles, bangers and Catherine wheels. French customs had no objection to the legally obtained fireworks leaving the country in bulk as it was keeping the local economy going. Their Irish counterparts were clever enough to look the other way, not fancying challenging a herd of Holy Joe street dealers from town. The fireworks would then be sold to offset the cost of the pilgrimage as well as paying a few essential bills and providing a couple of good nights out. Patrick smiled at the sight of the advancing women and the terrified pedestrians who had to almost dive out of the way to avoid being rammed. The chaos reminded him of his favourite cartoon, The Wacky Races, featuring Dick Dastardly and his sniggering dog, Muttley, as they unsuccessfully attempted to win various car races across America by hook or by crook.

"Howaya, love," Peggy, one of the street traders said in a raspy tone after spotting Patrick's mother.

"There ye are, Peggy," Mrs. Bridges warmly replied.

"I better leggit," said Peggy, "The bleedin' pigs are on me tail."

Patrick laughed out loud at his neighbour's rude referral to the Gardai but immediately stopped when he felt his mother giving his hand a gentle but firm squeeze.

"They've only gone and lagged poor aul Tony Gregory," Peggy informed her.

"Righ'," answered Mr. Bridges, completely shocked. She had a lot of time for their local T.D. and all the hard work he was doing for the community.

"They have him banged up in the Bridewell," continued Peggy.

"That's terrible," said Mrs. Bridges.

"I know. They have our hearts poxy broke, chasin' us around town like criminals and the kip bein' flooded with heroin," Peggy said, unable to hide her disgust.

Mrs. Bridges nodded sympathetically. She'd seen firsthand the way some of the local teenagers had been turned into zombies almost overnight.

"I'm tellin' ye straight and may God be me witness," continued Peggy, blessing herself enthusiastically, "But if we didn't have the likes of Gregory and Christy Burke they would shit on us altogether."

Patrick wasn't used to hearing language, especially not from adults but he was thoroughly enjoying the feisty dealer's rant.

A woman with beautifully manicured nails painted blood red appeared out of nowhere and began to peruse Peggy's bananas. She tutted ever so softly before feeling one of the bananas and rolling it slightly between her fingers and thumb.

"Quite small," the woman said, disapprovingly.

Patrick couldn't help but notice Peggy's changing demeanour caused by the woman's antics. The picky customer tutted once more and that was one tut too many for the dealer.

"It's a banana, love. It won't get any bigger the more you play with it," Peggy said.

The look of horror on the pernickety woman's face was priceless. Mortified, she scurried away as quickly as she could, taking refuge in the crowd. Peggy beamed at her little victory and turned back to Mrs. Bridges who had also managed a smile.

"Are ye alrigh', love?" the fruit and veg dealer asked all of a sudden, "Ye don't look great if I'm bein' brutally honest."

"I'm grand, a bit under the weather is all," Mrs. Bridges replied, trying to deflect her neighbour's genuine concerns.

"Ye should get yerself down to the doctors, migh' need an aul tonic," said Peggy.

Mrs. Bridges forced a smile.

"Or a few glasses of stout. Ye migh' be low in Iron," Peggy added.

"Will do," Mrs. Bridges replied, knowing that her street trading neighbour meant well.

"Peggy, they're comin'," roared another pram pusher, alerting her friend to the impending presence of the 'boys in blue'.

"Ye better go or ye'll be joinin' Gregory in a cell," Mrs. Bridges warned.

Peggy looked down at Patrick and gave his cheek an affectionate squeeze.

"Look after yer Ma, son, she's the only one ye'll ever have."

In an instance she was gone, scarpering down the street to join her fleeing, fugitive dealers.

"Why are the police chasin' Peggy and her friends, have they done somethin' wrong?" Patrick innocently asked.

"No, son. They're only tryin' to make a livin' like their people before them but the government won't give them any licences," his mother half explained.

This made absolutely no sense to Patrick and he wanted to know more but his mother said she was in a hurry to get to the hardware shop before it closed and that they'd chat about it later on.

Mrs. Bridges winced as she climbed the concrete stairwell of the neglected flats complex. This was a once proud community sadly ignored by myopic government policies despite numerous protests from local councillors over the years. The area seemed to be following in that all too familiar pattern that other parts of the city had experienced whereby council housing was left to go to rack and ruin and police presence became nonexistent leading to an upsurge in crime. The unhappy tenants would then be split up and moved out further into soulless estates on the outskirts. Developers would snap up the abandoned properties for half nothing with the promise of delivering a favourable percentage of affordable social housing. Time would pass and it would no longer be financially viable to provide this type of dwelling so a one off fee would be paid by the developer to the council instead and the housing list would in turn continue to grow. A community activist had explained it at a residents' meeting one time as a policy of 'managed decline' and warned that they were following in the footsteps of what Thatcher and her Tory government had done to the ordinary decent people of Liverpool. Most of Mrs. Bridges' neighbours found the concept very difficult to comprehend. It wasn't that they were stupid but they couldn't understand how any government in their right mind would do this to their own people. It just didn't make sense. Patrick heard some of the residents referring to the C word in their description of the passionate activist and he had asked his mother what they'd meant. Mrs. Bridges kindly explained that the man had been called a C for communist due to his political beliefs but despite this he was still a very good person and cared an awful lot about the community. Another relentless wave of pain bulldozed its way through her weakening body and she had to pause momentarily to grip the metal handrail, fearing that she might actually fall over. Patrick felt his mother sway and immediately clutched the material belt that was stitched onto her coat. She forced a smile as he helped her to step over an inebriated drunk who had wet himself.

"And yer gonna be alrigh'?" Patrick asked, immune to the increasing homeless situation blighting this part of the city.

Mrs. Bridges ruffled her son's hair.

"Yer not to be worryin', the doctor said that the pain will be gone in no time at all," she lied.

Patrick sat across from his Ma at the cheap flat-pack table which was a gift from a neighbour who was upgrading after finding herself a rich fancy man. Not surprisingly the new table lasted far longer than the bloke once his cash had ran out. A plate heaped with a generous amount of mashed potatoes smothered in gravy and with baked beans and sausages on the side was placed in front of him.

"This tastes a bit funny," he offered, after chewing on a mouthful of spuds.

"Nonsense, it's all in yer head," his Ma said, "And don't be talkin' with yer mouth full either."

Patrick felt guilty and immediately said, "Sorry."

"We don't want yer Da lookin' down from heaven and thinkin' yer a loser now, do we?"

The youngster glanced over at the imitation silver framed photograph of his late father which was sitting in a place of prominence on the mantelpiece.

"No, Ma," he respectfully answered.

"Ye can take me for a spin round the floor later on when ye digest yer food," Mrs. Bridges said, trying to lighten the mood.

Patrick couldn't help but smile. He would never admit it to anyone but he loved to dance. Not the Billie Barry type of stuff. No, a classic waltz would do him just fine. He'd kick off his shoes before carefully standing on his mother's slipper clad feet as she led him twirling and spinning round the room in fits of laughter. She loved to dance too, always had.

Patrick struggled to remember the last time they'd put on the old records and taken a tour of the room but he was chuffed that she was feeling much better.

The curtains were drawn closed even though it was still bright outside giving a supernatural quality to the darkened room while The Mamas and The Papas belted out their hit, California Dreamin' in the background. Mrs. Bridges grimaced as she tore strips from the large roll of the adhesive tape she'd acquired earlier from the hardware store and continued to seal the doorframe. Patrick was sat upright on the couch, covered with a fluffy duvet his mother had picked up in the bargain basement of a large department store nearby. His eyes were shut and he wore a peaceful, almost angelic smile. His mother shuffled past to the adjoining kitchen and turned on all the gas cooker knobs before heading back into the living-room. On the countertop next to the hissing rings lay an empty tablet container that recently housed sleeping pills filled to the brim. Mrs. Bridges collected the framed photograph of her late husband from the mantelpiece and carried it over to where her son soundly slept. She got under the duvet and snuggled in beside him while holding the photograph tight to her bosom.

"Sweet dreams," she whispered as a solitary tear escaped from the corner of her tired and bloodshot eye.

Chapter 2

Dublin - Present Day… Saturday.

The smartly dressed man in the dark pinstripe suit stood in stark contrast to the leafy green poster of the Amazon Rainforest which was taped to the wall behind him. He worked the scissors with the dull blade hard eventually cutting his way through the plastic ring which he'd removed from around the cap of a milk carton. The severed piece of plastic was promptly dispatched into an almost empty bin. After seeing some poor bird on a nature programme with its head stuck through something similar he'd made a conscious note to do his bit. Every little helps and all that lark. He then went to the bathroom and leaned towards the small cabinet mirror, scrutinizing his reflection. He frowned. Using a tweezers from the relatively sparse shelf, he plucked the tiniest of hairs from his left eyebrow. A smile swept across his face as he gave himself a mischievous wink.

"Perfect," he mouthed.

The sign above the swanky high street store read Kingsley Electrical. Inside, an harassed looking Mr. Kingsley spoke slowly but firmly to his latest assistant. He'd gone through at least half a dozen new employees in the last year alone and none of them had made it beyond the two month mark, the snowflakes. Hopefully this one would buck the trend and at least he didn't seem obsessed with taking Selfies or needing to post stories on his various social media accounts every five minutes.

"So you know how everything works?" he firmly repeated.

"Yes, Mr. Kingsley," Brian said, nodding obediently.

The boss couldn't help but notice the gangly employee's prominent Adam's apple and skin bearing numerous reminders of bouts of aggressive teen acne.

"I'll be gone thirty minutes at the very most," the shop owner said.

"Take all the time you want, Mr. K, I've got this," said the young assistant, giving what he thought was a reassuring wink.

Mr. Kingsley narrowed his eyes and grunted. He was about to chastise his employee for referring to him as Mr. K but decided to let it slip. There were more important matters in hand like satisfying his ever expanding stomach. He left the shop but not before looking back over his shoulder half a dozen times.

"Just as well I'll be long dead if that's the future," he grumbled to himself.

Brian strolled over to a full length mirror and checked out his reflection. Although the Windsor knot on his tie didn't particularly need adjusting he still felt the need to fiddle about with it. He'd bumped into an elderly couple he knew on his way to work and they'd wished him the best of luck in court. Before he could explain that he'd gotten a job they were already gone on their merry way, promising to say a prayer that he got off.

"Good afternoon, sir," Brian said aloud to the man in the mirror but immediately shook his head in disappointment.

Straightening his shoulders and puffing out his chest, he tried again only this time in a much deeper and hopefully more commanding tone. "Good afternoon, sir and how may I be of assistance?"

"Not bad. Yer first day?" asked a cheerful voice from behind.

Brian, mortified, swung round to find the smartly dressed man in the pinstripe suit standing there staring back at him.

"It's my second day actually," Brian answered honestly.

The man leaned in closer to the shop assistant and read his name badge.

"Well, Brian, ye definitely look the part," he complimented.

"Thank you," the shop assistant replied, reddening slightly. He wasn't used to getting compliments. In school he was constantly being referred to as a waste of space and that he'd never amount to anything.

The customer continued to stare making an awkward situation even more so. He eventually opened his mouth, breaking the silence.

"Well?" he asked.

"Sorry?" said Brian.

The customer smiled and asked, "Are ye not going to offer me your expert help?"

"Oh yeah, sorry about that," Brian said, smiling goofily. "Good afternoon, sir and how may I be of assistance?"

"Not bad. Not bad at all. D'ye work on a commission basis?" the customer asked.

Brian's eyes lit up brighter than the Blackpool illuminations.

Less than thirty minutes later the smartly dressed gentleman had spent the guts of ten thousand euro and he wasn't finished yet.

"Give us a quick rundown like a good lad," he requested.

Brian picked up the order book where he had written the extensive list of items and reeled them off back to the customer all the while thinking to himself that if 'Carlsberg did customers...' He also thought it very peculiar that a shop selling the most modern and up to-date technology would be using a pen and paper to record orders but he'd said nothing to his boss. Mr. Kingsley might have been old school but he was definitely nobody's fool. Scribbling away on paper allowed him to adjust the orders later on and to only input the minimum amount of sales thus avoiding hefty taxes. Life was one big fiddle and he could definitely hold his own tune with the best of them and besides, he'd paid more than his fair share over the years unlike the shysters making the rules.

"Better make it another ninety-inch flat screen tv with the cinema surround sound thingamajigs, in case herself wants to watch her soaps while the footy's on," laughed the big spending customer.

"Or maybe you'll be the one looking at the soaps while your partner's watching the football?" joked Brian, feeling really at ease with the customer.

The man in the suit laughed again and said, "Touché, brother, touché."

Brian beamed, delighted with his own cleverness. He totted up in his head the handsome commission he was going to earn.

"That's us all sorted then," the customer said, "I've a few important deals need closin' in the financial services centre and then I'll be righ' back to collect the stuff and to sort out payment."

"No worries, I'll have it all ready and waiting, sir," said the eager assistant.

The satisfied customer smiled and left the shop leaving Brian fist pumping the air, dreaming of a sun holiday with the lads and with any luck, finally losing his virginity.

A pristine, black Mercedes was parked at the base of one of the graffiti covered blocks of flats. In contrast, a partially burnt out car was abandoned only yards away. Young boys were jumping up and down on the roof of the battered vehicle while others smashed what was left of the windows with iron bars causing an awful racket. Several floors above the commotion in a cramped living-room sat a woman named Janice. Premature lines were etched into her taut but pretty face and although her eyes were tired they couldn't quite mask a genuine kindness. She was perched on the edge of an armchair, subconsciously playing with a wedding ring that had loosened slightly in recent weeks. Frank Harris, middle-aged and dressed in a smart, tailor made double-breasted suit, lounged comfortably on the couch opposite. He flicked through a thick copybook easily obtained from any stationary shop worth its salt. His powerfully built minder was seated next to him wearing a stupid grin. Janice spied her two young children out of the corner of her eye attempting to sneak into the room.

"Out, kids and do yer homework or somethin'," she said, scolding her son and daughter. She wasn't normally like this but she'd been up to ninety of late and was doing her best just to stay afloat.

Frank looked up from his copybook and said, "Let them stay, they might learn a thing or two about how the real world works."

Janice knew there was no point in protesting. The children hurriedly climbed up onto the sides of the armchair and snuggled in beside their mother. Frank resumed flicking through his ledger. The minder lifted his polished, leather shoes and plonked them down on the coffee table much to Janice's chagrin and she couldn't let it go.

"Take yer feet off me table," she demanded, glaring at the muscled-bound hulk.

The minder flatly ignored the woman's request.

"That's not strictly true now, is it?" Frank said, correcting Janice without looking up from his paperwork. "I mean, by my reckoning I must own at least half of it."

The minder blew Janice a kiss and her children stared at her to see how she'd react but she kept her cool, at least on the outside. Frank glanced at his henchman.

"Get your shoes off of our table," he instructed with a steely tone.

The minder immediately did as he was told and although he said nothing, Janice glimpsed a flash of resentment wash over him. Frank held a page open in his ledger and slowly ran his index finger along a line that contained several figures inked in red.

"Enough of the idle chit-chat," he said, "Let's get down to business. You still owe me ten grand so why should I give you anymore?"

"Like I was tellin' ye. There's a manager's job goin' and the money will be a lot better..." she began before being interrupted by Frank.

"And what makes you think your that special you'll be offered the position?" he snidely asked, "Unless of course the boss is giving you one on the side?"

The minder smirked while Janice did her best to ignore the ignorant remark. She was grateful that the slur had gone over her innocent children's heads.

"I've been workin' there for five years now, the other girl was only taken on a few months ago," Janice explained.

"I don't know..." Frank said, toying with the desperate woman's emotions.

"Please, Mr. Harris. I've got to get them outta this kip," Janice pleaded, "Ye know I'll be good for it."

Frank brushed away an imaginary speck of dirt from his designer suit trousers, purposely delaying things so as to emphasise his own self importance. After a few moments he sat forward and looked Janice directly into her sad eyes and said, "It was a bit inconvenient the way your old man popped his clogs like that, saddling you with all his bad debts."

Janice bit down hard on her lower lip. She wanted to scream at this scumbag who was sucking the very life out of her and what remained of her family but she held back. She wasn't going to give him the pleasure.

"Alright, but I'm only doing it for the kids," Frank conceded with a wave of his hand in some grandiose gesture.

"Thanks Mr. Harris, I won't let ye down," she immediately replied.

The gangster smirked and said, "Oh I know you won't, Janice." He didn't need to spell it out. He held open the palm of his enormous hand. The minder hastily produced a substantial wad of cash from an inside jacket pocket and passed it over.

A homeless man in his early sixties with a face tanned and weathered from endless days exposed to the elements, sat on the pavement outside Flynn's mini-mart. His back rested against the rough wall of the shop while a folded piece of cardboard offered a small bit of comfort between the cold concrete and his scrawny backside. Inside the premises, Mick, the burly shopkeeper with the almost eternal sourpuss, stormed up to the counter where Janice was restocking cigarettes into their separate, see-through compartments.

"He's out there again. You need to get rid of him, now," he demanded, nodding towards the large window.

Janice threw her eyes to the ceiling in what Mick wrongly believed to be a show of solidarity.

Janice emerged from the shop and smiled sadly at the homeless man, thinking of the many hardships he had to endure. She knew very little about him other than his name was Larry, he was extremely polite and that he also had a sweet tooth. It really frightened her to think that this could very well be the future for her and her young children but she was adamant that she would do everything in her power to prevent it. She bent down next to the man, checked back over her shoulder before producing a jam doughnut and a polystyrene cup of tea.

"The blessings of God on ye, Janice," thanked Larry.

"Yer more than welcome, love. Ye better make yerself scarce though, he's threatenin' to call the Guards again," she warned.

By the time Janice had gone back into the shop following her good deed Mick had already filled a plastic bucket with hot steaming water and was emptying the entire contents of a bottle of bleach into it. Janice totted up the cost of the tea and doughnut on the till, discreetly retrieved money from her own pocket and paid for Larry's two items. When she looked around the shopkeeper had disappeared but returned almost immediately with a deck scrub. He glanced over at Tina, his stunning new employee who was preoccupied with blowing onto her freshly painted nails. After a couple of seconds she looked up and realised what her boss was indicating. She immediately pulled a face as if to say 'are you for real?' Mick gave a stupid grin before turning to good old reliable Janice instead.

As Janice diligently cleansed the outside pavement with the deck scrub, a customer hurried past cheerfully wishing her a 'good morning'. She looked up but the man had already entered the shop. A thin woman in her late sixties with a sharp nose and an even sharper countenance ambled along an aisle closely followed by Mick. It wasn't that he suspected her of shoplifting, he knew the security camera hanging from the ceiling captured everything. No, he was growing more irate as the woman picked up various items from the neatly stacked rows, scrutinised the ingredients before putting them back again, any which way. The pernickety shopkeeper followed her around, fixing the replaced items ensuring that the labels were pointing perfectly outwards. After several minutes of this cat and mouse type scenario the woman stopped dead in her tracks and glared at Mick but he quickly turned away not having the stomach for confrontation. The customer exhaled loudly, left the shop without purchasing anything all the while shaking her head in complete bewilderment. Once she was gone Mick repositioned the last item that she had moved. Over at the till Tina was serving the cheerful man who had entered only moments earlier.

"Five-euro," she said, tossing a printed lotto slip onto the counter.

The man counted out a bunch of coins of varying values oblivious to Tina's scornful expression.

"Thanks," he said, handing over the change and pocketing the ticket. He then turned and bounded out of the shop.

The imposing London plane trees which lined both sides of the broad street offered partial respite from the dazzling sunlight. Underneath the leafy canopy, the man sauntered along with his jacket draped over his left shoulder and a plastic bag from his local off-license swinging from his right hand. 'Ye'd never want to leave the country if ye were guaranteed weather like this,' he thought to himself. He had read an article recently about some crowd putting a roof over a forest up the country and building a theme park or a gigantic swimming pool under it. Now that was using your eight ounces. As he approached the imposing Georgian building he started to whistle one of his favourite tunes, ABBA's Money, Money, Money. There was a gentle resistance from the ornate metal gate accompanied by a muffled whine which always reminded him of the brass band he'd once heard playing in the local park when he was a boy. He returned the gate to its latch with a shove, took the darkened granite steps two at a time then went searching in his trouser pocket for his hall door key.

Mr. Kingsley had decided to indulge in a few small ones to wash down his extended pub lunch. Although his wife had warned him to cut back and to watch his cholesterol he had succumbed to the delicious roast pork on offer. He'd also sampled all the trimmings including a couple of Yorkshire puddings smothered in gravy followed by a tasty trifle for good measure. Stuffed to the gills he waddled back to his shop in far better spirits than when he had left. There was no point in working hard all your life if you couldn't afford a few little perks he'd convinced himself. Brian, his gangly assistant, was positioned behind the till wearing a lopsided grin that only a mother could love on payday.

"There you are, lad. At least you didn't manage to burn the place down in my absence then," Mr. Kingsley joked as he glanced around the premises none the less just to make sure.

Brian gave a small chuckle while nodding enthusiastically. He handed over the order book as if he was offering up the Fourth Secret of Fatima. His boss read through the extensive list of items that had been sold. Brian watched closely, waiting for the praise that was surely going to be bestowed upon him.

"Patrick Bridges," Mr. Kingsley muttered in a barely audible voice while slowly shaking his head. He then abruptly tore the page from the order book, scrunched it up into a ball and threw it into the air. As it plummeted back to earth he kicked it across the room almost toppling over.

Brian put a hand to the side of his faced and gaped at the unfolding spectacle.

"He's a Walter Mitty," Mr. Kingsley said by way of an explanation. "I'll be in my office in case of an emergency such as a nuclear attack or something worse." He made his way towards the back of the shop, shoulders slumped, his earlier good humour having all but vanished.

'There goes the ride in Santa Ponsa,' thought Brian.

There was a feeling of being entombed as the enormous hall door closed behind Patrick Bridges, shutting out the last of the sunshine from the unusually bright day. With no windows and a twelve foot high ceiling, the hallway of the Georgian House suddenly grew cold. His whistling ceased. He looked around at the peeling wallpaper and the worn, dull carpet. Trying his best not to let the gloom get in the way of his earlier optimism he attempted to focus his energies on what was hopefully going to be the night that changed the rest of his life, forever. He had no sooner placed his foot on the bottom step to begin his ascent when he suddenly stiffened. Loud banging echoed from the landing above.

"I know you're in there, Bridges, you little pup," shouted the landlord as he continued to bash on the door with a closed fist.

Patrick calmly turned round and ducked into a cupboard under the stairs.

The landlord had his hands planted on his hips, panting heavily, his exertions getting the better of him. He glared at the door to bedsit 2B.

"You have until Wednesday, you fecking parasite, do you hear me?" he roared. He then gave the door a kick for good measure. "Then you're out, I swear. And another thing, the brother's a detective in Store Street, I can get you arrested in a flash if I want."

Patrick rested on an upturned plastic bin in the sanctuary of the cupboard, casually picking his nails clean and deciding to wait this one out. Sounds resembling a stampeding bull thundering down the stairs rang out as the frustrated landlord, his tantrum almost fizzling out, stormed towards the exit.

"Next Wednesday, do you hear me?" he shouted. The hall door was slammed shut knocking off a piece of plaster from the already crumbling walls.

Cautious of being tricked, Patrick remained seated for a further five minutes until he was convinced that the coast was clear. He popped his head out slightly and listened carefully for several seconds. When he was fully satisfied that it was safe to leave his hidey-hole he coolly proceeded to climb the stairs to his flat.

Bedsit 2B was sparsely furnished with cheap bits and pieces mostly scavenged from skips. It never ceased to amaze Patrick what some people classed as rubbish. He'd often rescue a retro looking chair, a bedside locker or even a framed poster of some obscure band all of which he was able to offload, for a tidy profit, to a lad he knew with a stall down the local flea market. An eighties styled ghetto-blaster and a television set that wouldn't have looked out of place in a museum decorated the room. Patrick removed a bottle of sparkling cider from his plastic off-license bag, gave it a kiss then carefully placed it inside an otherwise lonely fridge. He then flicked on the immersion before taking off his suit jacket and hanging it in a door-less wardrobe. His Rolex watch which was really a knockoff from Taiwan was unclasped and carefully deposited on the window ledge as if it was the real deal. Once he'd arrived home he no longer felt the need to keep up the charade of looking important. He picked up a cylindrical cardboard container of fish food, popped open the lid and gave it a quick sniff. Although he recoiled from the smell it still brought back pleasant memories of his very early childhood. He smiled as he recalled the time when he was in the newly opened pet shop on Capel Street in the heart of the city with his Da, looking at the tropical fish. It was a wondrous place and the closest thing he was ever going to get to the deep sea adventures which his hero Jacques Cousteau regularly went on. Several other customers were also admiring the display when his Da suddenly plunged his hand into one of the tanks and pulled out a wriggling goldfish. He then proceeded to gobble it down as the horrified customers looked on while also retreating several steps. A blonde lady with an enormous bouffant and an even bigger handbag began to gag, something Patrick's Da found quite entertaining. Patrick remembered being tongue-tied as he was quickly led outside by his giggling parent. They legged it down the street and around a corner before slowing to a brisk walk. He remembered his father glancing back over his shoulder then looking down at him, a mischievous grin lighting up his face and making him look several years younger.

"That was a bit of gas, wasn't it," his Da had said, almost out of breath. "I could do with a pint to get rid of the taste though. C'mon."

Shortly after their pet shop escapades Patrick was ushered into a dark and smoky aul lads' pub where he was hoisted into the air and gently deposited onto a high stool. An elderly Jack Russell lying close-by at the feet of its owner lifted its head slightly and eyeballed the pair. Satisfied that there wasn't any immediate threat the dog rested its chin on its front paws and closed its eyes.

"A pint of Guinness and a glass of red lemonade for the youngfella," Patrick's Da said.

The barman sized up the pair of them before replying, "We only have Fanta."

Patrick's Da looked at his son, unsure.

"Is that okay with you?" he asked.

"Yes, thanks," Patrick politely answered, delighted with any sort of a treat. And in anyway, Fanta was his actual favourite.

The barman went about his business of pulling the pint and fetching the fizzy orange while the stout was settling.

Try as he might, Patrick couldn't help but stare at his Da. He couldn't believe that he'd eaten a live fish when he was always preaching about being kind to poor innocent animals.

"Can I ask ye a question?" Patrick eventually plucked up the courage to say.

"Fire away, son," said his Da, while sneaking a glance at his pint of Guinness to see how it was coming along.

"Wha' did it taste like?" the young boy asked.

His father looked up to the ceiling, pursed his lips and wrinkled his brow as he gave the question some serious consideration. After a few moments he looked the boy squarely in the eyes and said, "Vegetables."

Patrick beamed in amazement. Of all the things he

would have imagined that a goldfish might taste of he would never have guessed vegetables.

"More specifically, carrots," his father added.

"Carrots?" repeated Patrick.

His father then proceeded to take a carrot out of his jacket pocket which he'd earlier cut into the shape of a goldfish and giddily wiggled it about in the air. Patrick shrieked with delight causing some of the older men in the pub to glance up from their pints of stout with disapproving scowls. The Jack Russell wasn't impressed either. Mr. Bridges gave his son a playful wink and ruffled his hair as he handed over the pretend fish for him to eat. Patrick laughed as he momentarily recalled the happy memory but his mood soon quickly changed. He also remembered his Da slipping out of the pub and promising to be back in a tick only to reappear over an hour later with a defeated expression on his face. The barman had looked sternly at Mr. Bridges not bothering to hide his disgust. This had greatly surprised Patrick as the man had been very kind to him, giving him free lemonade and a couple of bags of the crisps, the ones in those expensive tinfoil packets, while he patiently waited for his father to return.

Patrick and his Dad had walked home in silence and although the boy knew something was wrong he didn't dare ask. He thought it might have had something to do with the pet shop until he'd heard his parents arguing later that evening about his father squandering money again in the bookies. He gave a wry smile before measuring out a quantity of the finely chopped flakes into a large pickled onion jar that he'd converted into a fish bowl. He'd scrubbed it thoroughly with his toothbrush, getting into all the nooks and crannies to make sure it was nice and clean. He was then forced to replace the toothbrush the following day after he'd gotten the unmistakeable the taste of onions while cleaning his teeth. The solitary goldfish immediately made a beeline for the surface and began to gobble up all the food in sight.

"Did I hear somethin'?" Patrick suddenly asked, looking round before setting his sights on a vigorous looking Venus flytrap plant loitering on the window-ledge. "What's that?" he asked, cupping a hand over one ear and moving towards the potted plant. "Feed me, Seymour," he said aloud, "Feed me now." He shook his head, pointed at the potted plant and said, "I told ye, Mallet Head, me name's Patrick not Seymour." He picked up a set of chopsticks lying on the window-ledge and stalked a fly which was zig-zagging madly up and down against the glass trying desperately to escape. With the stealth of a viper, at least that was the vision he had in his own head, he struck and expertly caught the insect. "Eat yer heart out, Mr. Miyagi," he said, delighted with his own dexterity. The fly was immediately dispatched into the gaping 'mouth' of the carnivorous plant triggering its expectant jaws. Despite the insect's best efforts it couldn't escape as Mallet Head clamped down harder. "Ye don't know how lucky ye are, bein' fed free range flies like that. Spoilt rotten so ye are."

In the bedsit directly below Patrick's, a young couple named Tommy and Debbie were lounging on their battered leather couch, a 'gift' from Debbie's uncle who was chucking the thing out. With an assortment of cartons from the local Chinese takeaway resting on lap trays and a couple of freshly opened cans of lager in hand, the couple were settling down for the big movie. Debbie had picked it out and it was probably going to be a load of shite but Tommy didn't care. He idolised the ground on which his new bride walked. Sudden loud music pumping from the upstairs flat caused the couple to arch their heads towards the ceiling at almost the same time. Tommy then turned to Debbie.

"Pass us the remote, love," he said.

ABBA's 'The Winner Takes It All' was belting out of the ghetto-blaster that was straight out of the eighties causing the bedsits paper thin windowpane to vibrate in tandem. Patrick, now dressed casually in a track bottoms and t-shirt, was busting a few moves as he sang along to the Swedish quartet while drying his hair with a threadbare towel.

La la la la la la,
La la la la la la.

He imagined a God nonchalantly throwing a dice watched by his disinterested peers, deciding someone's fate back on earth. 'Cruel feckers but a belter of a tune all the same,' he thought.

Finished with the towel, he leaned forward onto his tippy toes and deftly threw it, landing it perfectly into the laundry basket. "Get in there ye good thing," he said aloud. He glanced over at his goldfish. "Due the big one tonigh', Jaws. Get ye a bigger pad then, I promise." He manually switched his T.V. on then flopped down onto his single bed with the squeaky springs not that there'd been much squeaking of late. A glossy holiday brochure along with several photos of expensive looking houses were pulled out from under him and placed on the floor. On screen a reporter who was a ringer for Beaker from the Muppets was quizzing an official from the National Lottery.

"So tell us again, for the benefit of those viewers who may have been living on Mars for the last thirty years. How does it work?" the reporter asked in an upbeat manner.

The lottery official wasn't sure if he was supposed to face the reporter or look directly into the camera and his discomfort was obvious. Beaker was well accustomed to this sort of thing. He gave his companion a reassuring smile and nodded his head encouragingly.

The lottery man then cleared his throat and said, "Basically, you can either pick your six numbers from one to forty-seven or you can let the machine select them for you..."

"And that would be a 'quick pick?'" the reporter interjected.

"Correct," said the lottery man. "The balls are released into a clear spinning drum, for transparency of course, and then six are randomly chosen."

Beaker nodded enthusiastically and listened intently as if this was the first time he'd ever heard this spiel. His lips pursed and relaxed as if they were doing some sort of independent exercise while the odd nod of agreement was thrown in for good measure.

"And this is done twice weekly?" he then asked.

"Yes, Wednesdays and Saturdays."

"And can you tell us a little bit about the good causes which the Lotto supports?"

The lottery official's eyes lit up. Although the state had sold off the rights to a foreign consortium, the powers that be liked to project the idea that it was like one big massive savings scheme for the Irish public.

"Ninety percent of lottery sales are returned to communities in the form of prizes, good causes and commission to retailers," he said.

Beaker didn't look in the least bit convinced but kept quiet.

"In the past few years we have helped fund projects as diverse as say your local gardening club to the National Aquatics Centre," the lottery man added.

The reporter gave a cheesy chuckle and said, "You've also helped to create a few millionaires along the way?"

"We have indeed. Three in the last week alone and well over nine hundred since we began in nineteen eighty-seven believe it or not."

Patrick shot forward on his bed and shouted at the television, "Ye can add another one to that list tonigh', pal."

Although there were plans afoot to have all of the street lighting upgraded with LED bulbs before the year was out, a considerable amount of streets had still remained untouched, not that everyone was complaining. The older, murkier lighting made it much easier for the nefarious activities which went on beneath them. Billy and his delinquent crew was one such gang who took full advantage of the poor lighting, dealing mostly in hash and skunk. Business had been brisk by the time the black Mercedes rolled up next to the kerb. Billy and his mates immediately recognised the car as belonging to Frank Harris and cautiously approached. The driver's window was lowered and the minder's big head appeared. He glared at his audience and spotted the man he wanted. Billy was beckoned closer by the minder's sausage-like index finger. The thug did as he was ordered but not before throwing a few shapes along the way. Image was everything on the streets. He casually rested his hand on the door but immediately knew it was a mistake. The minder grabbed it, squeezing it tightly. Billy knew better than to struggle even though it felt as if his bones were being crushed to powder. The minder glared at the rest of the gang.

"Piss off," he said, not bothering to hide the disdain which he felt for them. In his mind he was premier league where as these lowlifes were non league at best.

The young thugs duly obliged without so much as a word, retreating into the darkness like the cockroaches they were. Satisfied that he had been obeyed, the minder released his grip on Billy. The thug breathed a sigh of relief and dropped his hand out of sight so that he could try and wriggle some life back into his fingers. He reached inside his jacket with his good hand, retrieved a substantial wad of cash and passed it over.

"It's all there," he said.

Frank gave a menacing smile. "Ah fair play, and sure if it's not we can always call back later and shoot you in the face."

Billy gave a compliant nod having heard enough stories. The minder handed him a small see-through plastic packet containing a rose-grey coloured powder. Frank leaned forward, his eyes cold and filled with malice.

"Try not to stick into your veins all in the one go," he said patronisingly as if speaking to a young child about sweets.

Billy ran his tongue along the outside of his lower gum in anticipation much to Frank's disgust.

"Keep your phone on," the gangster said, "I'll have a few more errands for you to run."

The minder smirked at Billy then raised the window. Moments later the Mercedes pulled away from the kerb and disappeared into the night, no doubt to bring more misery to some unfortunate community.

The kitchen window of the modest council house was partially open giving the cigarette smoke a chance to escape. Jackie and Tony, a couple in their mid thirties, were sat hunched over the table, sipping coffee and sucking the life out of almost spent cigarettes. An overflowing ashtray loitered between them. The front hall door opened and was banged shut moments later. Tony reached across the table, took hold of his worried partner's hand and gave it a gentle, reassuring squeeze.

"Are you gonna tell him or do ye want me to?" he asked in a low voice.

Before Jackie could answer Billy bounced into the room on a mad buzz.

"What's the story, Tony?" Billy greeted loudly.

"Howaya, Billy," Tony cautiously replied.

Billy looked at Jackie and said, "Any chocolate, sis, I'm bleedin' starvin'."

She snatched a sly look at Tony who glumly smiled in return.

Patrick was slouched on his bed with his hands resting behind his head and his good runners kicked off, close by. He'd picked them up for half nothing in a little sports shop he often frequented down by the quay and run by the friendly Sikh chap with the big smiley head. The stuff was always that bit cheaper because it was from last year's range, something that didn't bother Patrick in the least. Of course the younger, more hip people called them trainers or kicks or some shite like that nowadays and boasted about how much they'd spent. It was a far cry from when he was a youngfella growing up in the inner-city. He'd be delighted just to have been given a new pair of Sizzlers from Penneys. There was this one local lad, Crutchy Philips, who always wore the best of footwear. This drove the rest of the kids mad with jealousy. The fact that Crutchy had only one leg following a bad accident didn't come into the equation. His mother was always going around bragging at every opportunity that her son only wore the latest fashion. She neglected to mention that she robbed the samples off of the display shelves but everyone knew. Most of the locals weren't adverse to a small bit of shoplifting but they didn't like their noses being rubbed in it and were delighted when the shoe shops finally copped on, albeit after a tip off, and started putting out the right foot instead. A celebratory bottle of sparkling cider with accompanying plastic flute waited on a side locker, constructed out of laminated chipboard which Patrick had found dumped outside the building one morning. He'd also found a selection of screws and it was obvious that someone had lost their flat-pack battle and probably the will to live into the bargain. The familiar lotto music began to play on the television.

"And tonight's jackpot stands at four million, eight hundred and fifty two thousand euro," the presenter announced.

Patrick jumped up and retrieved his cumbersome, square-shaped glasses from his suit jacket which were almost identical to the ones he wore as a boy. He flopped back down onto the bed, rubbed his hands gleefully together and glanced over at his goldfish.

"That'll just about do us, Jaws, wha'?"

On screen the lotto balls were released into the spinning drum.

The couple in the flat below had snuggled closer, engrossed in the surprisingly good thriller which Debbie had chosen. The terrified child on screen was hiding in the closet from the axe wielding murderer and was peeking through a tiny crack in the closet. The menacing figure passed by with a bloodied axe resting on his shoulder tricking the audience into thinking that the child was going to be okay. The killer suddenly swung round and the axe was sent smashing through the flimsy door, showering the petrified child with timber splinters. At that precise moment a scream that would put the hairs on the back of your neck jolting upright and send your heart sideways, was heard coming from Patrick's bedsit. Needless to say both Tommy and his partner Debbie leapt several inches off of their couch. Debbie held her chest while staring up at the ceiling as the sounds of glass breaking, voices shouting and several loud thuds followed.

"Jaysus, Tommy, you'd better get up there quick and see what's goin' on," she urged, fearing the worst for their neighbour.

Tommy rolled his tongue round the inside of his cheek giving him time to evaluate the situation. "I'll give it a minute, if it continues I'll go up," he replied. It wasn't that he was afraid but he didn't want to walk in on another man's grief if he could help it. He'd heard enough stories over the years of blokes intervening in domestics only for the couple to turn on them. Instead, he tried to focus on the telly while taking a generous sip from his can of lager.

His partner couldn't relax and continued to stare at the ceiling.

"Guaranteed he's havin' a row with his mot or somethin' like that," Tommy suggested.

Debbie wasn't convinced however as the raised muffled voices continued to argue above.

"She's long gone," she said, absently.

"Wha' was that?" asked Tommy.

"The tramp he was seein', the one who made a pass at you?" Debbie said, still raging at the incident which happened a few months back. "She's gone off the scene."

Tommy put his arm around his partner's shoulders and gently eased her in closer to him. "In anyway, it seems to be quietenin' down now," he said. He raised the volume on the television hoping that the agro above would quickly blow over.

Fragments of glass from where the bottle of sparkling cider had gone through Patrick's television littered the floor. His bed was upturned and thrown into a corner with one of the legs hanging limply. He sat on the ground with his head in his hands, crying softly. His unsuccessful lottery ticket, now torn to shreds, lay scattered like confetti amongst the crumpled holiday brochures and discarded photos of expensive properties. Just like his lotto ticket, his dreams were now also in pieces.

Across the city things weren't going too well for Jackie and Tony either. The couple were backed into a corner with Jackie sheltering behind Tony, shaking like a leaf and sobbing her heart out. The couple had lived a lie for so many years and although it was never their intention to hurt anyone they knew that the revelation would ultimately cause immense pain. They only hoped that as a family they could work their way through the situation and finally make things right. Billy however was having none of it. Being as high as a kite hadn't helped the teenager to process the bombshell which Tony had dropped.

"No, no, no! Me Ma and Da are dead," Billy shouted, continuing to strut back and forth across the confined kitchen. He stopped suddenly and pointed at the petrified couple. "Yer me sister and he's, he's just yer fella." He grabbed hold of a frying pan sitting on the cooker and forcefully flung it through the window, smashing it to pieces.

"We wanted to tell ye before..." Tony said.

"When the time was righ'..." said Jackie.

"When the time was fuckin' righ'!" Billy roared, "Howaya, Billy, I'm not really yer sister I'm yer Ma. And ye know Tony? Only he's not just me fella, he's also yer Da."

He squared up to the couple and raised a tightly clenched fist. Nobody uttered a word for a few seconds. Billy finally shook his tormented head, turned on his heels and bounced back out of the room making sure to slam the door as hard as he could on his way out.

Chapter 3

Sunday.

Janice had her first Sunday off from work in God knew how
long and decided to bring her children up to visit their late
father's grave. Not that she'd ever admit it to anyone but she'd
felt so angry when her husband had taken his own life and
had left her and the kids to deal with the fallout, alone. She
had urged him time and again to get help with his gambling
addiction and had even threatened to leave him, not that
she ever would, but it always fell on deaf ears. She clenched
her fists tightly and ordered herself to get a grip and to put a
brave face on things for the sake of the children. They'd been
through enough shit as it was, losing their Dad who apart
from his addiction was always a very loving and caring man.

"Let's go," she cheerily said, ushering her kids towards
the front door.

They did as they were told without a single word of
complaint, perhaps picking up on their mother's underlying
feelings. Janice had had to spin them a few white lies the
previous evening about Frank Harris and his ignorant
associate after their visit to the flat but she knew they were
still a little concerned.

"Hold on a sec," she said, nipping back into the living-
room and retrieving the thick envelope filled with cash which
Frank the moneylender had loaned her. She looked around
for a good hiding place but couldn't think of anywhere

satisfactory. Instead, she stuffed the envelope deep inside her handbag. Although not really happy with her choice she was more afraid to leave it in the flat after a spate of recent burglaries in the area.

The Georgian House felt unusually lonely as Patrick trudged down steps which were unsurprisingly dimpled in the middle after taking the burden of a century's worth of footfall. Just as he approached the imposing front door, his downstairs neighbour, Tommy, entered the building with a folded newspaper neatly tucked under his arm. Their eyes met and an awkward silence ensued.

Tommy eventually broke the deadlock and said, "Not a bad mornin' all the same."

"Yeah? What's seldom is wonderful I suppose," Patrick politely answered.

The men had passed each other when Tommy turned round and said, "I hope ye don't think I'm bein' nosey or anythin' but is everythin' alrigh'?"

Patrick wore a blank expression. Tommy wished he'd kept his trap shut and just minded his own business but now that he'd started he felt he'd no choice but to continue.

"It's just that I was goin' to go up to ye last nigh', see if ye were in some sort of trouble like," he said.

Patrick's cheeks flushed.

"Oh, the noise and stuff. Yeah, sorry about that," he apologised. He'd been so caught up in his own rage that it never occurred to him how his actions might have negatively impacted on others. "Everything's great," he lied, "I lost me rag and smashed the flat up. Didn't win the lotto, again."

It was Tommy's turn to look embarrassed. He shuffled from one foot to the other wondering what he should do next.

Patrick then leaned forward and playfully threw an imaginary dig into Tommy's side.

"I'm only jokin', ye mad thing," he said, laughing. "Had a row with the ball and chain, ye know the score."

The neighbour shook his head slightly and gave a broad smile.

"Jaysus, ye had me goin' there," he said, "Thought ye were after losin' it."

"Oh that happened to me a long time ago, trust me," Patrick replied and duly left.

Glasnevin cemetery or the dead centre of Dublin as some of the city's old stock fondly called it had become a hip place to be nowadays. There seemed to be as much interest in genealogical research and guided walks as there was in the burying and burning aspect of things. It wasn't unusual to see people rambling around, sipping from takeaway coffee cups bought from the on-site restaurant, laughing and chatting as if they were strolling through a town park on a sunny day. In fairness to the people who maintained the place it had really come along since Patrick's visits as a child. The place had always reminded him of one of those nuclear disaster films where every bit of foliage was burnt to a crisp and the headstones were leaning at precarious angles as if hit by the aftershock. These days it was in pristine condition and a place of national pride although he knew his late Granny would have probably called it notions. Despite this new found interest in death, things were unusually quiet on this particular Sunday morning. Unsurprisingly, he was startled when he heard an apologetic male voice close behind him saying, "Sorry for disturbing you?"

Patrick turned round and was faced by a lanky chap with an enormous black, bushy beard which a pirate wouldn't have minded given an arm or a leg for or even an eye. The dude also wore a pleasant demeanour which softened the effect.

"Yer grand," Patrick said.

"I'm a bit lost and the app on my phone is acting up," the beardy chap said, glancing at his mobile.

"That's wha' happens when ye rely too much on technology," offered Patrick but not in a patronising manner.

Beardy gave an agreeable nod.

"I'm trying to find the resting place of Michael Collins?" he said.

"Yer not too far, bud," answered Patrick before pointing the way to a pathway running back towards the main entrance gates. "Straight up there and it's on yer left. Ye can't miss it, it's the one with all the flowers."

Beardy thanked Patrick and was on his way. Patrick doubted that even a single person would remember him when he departed this earth never mind the steady flow of visitor's which came to pay their respects to the legendary Irish rebel.

Two basic, small wooden crosses marked the grave where Patrick was hunkered. It belonged to his parents. One of the crosses was barely legible after years of weathering and read Patrick Bridges Snr. The other one wasn't much better and had Maggie Bridges crudely etched into it. Patrick flicked away a tear which had escaped from the corner of his eye.

"Yis are still here, wha'?" he said, trying to make light of the situation. "I could do with a bit of luck righ' now so I was just wonderin', if yis had the time like. Could ye ask the main man for a favour, more specifically next week's lotto numbers or the week after at the very least."

A few rows away, Janice stood over her late husband's grave with Jack and Emma waiting obediently by her side. Fresh daffodils rested on the weed-free earth. Jack turned his head to the side and noticed how sad Patrick looked. He picked up one of the daffodils and walked over to Patrick, holding out the flower.

Sensing a presence, Patrick looked up and was surprised to see the young boy. He quickly removed a handkerchief from his pocket and blew his nose.

"Did ye lose yer Da as well?" Jack kindly asked.

"Yeah, and me Ma too," said Patrick, his voice cracking slightly.

The young lad nodded and handed over the yellow flower.

"Thanks," Patrick said, feeling like the first time he'd watched the animated movie, Up. Jaysus, that film had really torn at his heartstrings, especially the opening scenes with the two kids.

Jack returned to his mother and was swallowed up in an enormous hug.

While Janice and her young family were paying their respects to their loved one, Billy the teenage tearaway was wandering aimlessly through the rows of headstones, still trying to get his head round what his sister, no, his fuckin' Ma had told him the previous night. He volleyed a glass vase containing artificial flowers into the cool summer air smashing it against an elaborate Celtic cross headstone with freshly engraved lettering. It never dawned on the thug how this simple act of vandalism might impact on the mourner who'd left the vase there in the first instance. As he was admiring his heroic kick he spotted Janice and her two young children standing in the near distance with their heads solemnly bowed. He was drawn towards the handbag which the woman was holding close to her body. With an evil smirk he pulled up his hood and hoped that maybe his run of bad luck was about to change.

With lightning speed and agility more akin to a practitioner of Parkour, that urban style of running and jumping, Billy darted across the uneven heaps of earth and snatched Janice's handbag. Although caught by surprise, she still managed to grab hold of the strap. A sly punch to the face knocked her off balance and she was violently dragged to the ground. She desperately continued to hold onto the bag and was given a kick full force into the kidneys for her troubles. The bag was then viciously reefed from her hand and the scumbag was gone, scarpering for a rusted iron fence less than fifty metres away.

Patrick's nostrils flared as he trudged back towards Janice who was now seated on the stone edging that surrounded her late husband's grave. Her face was buried deep in her hands with her shoulders jerking involuntarily. Jack and Emma flanked her on both sides, crying softly but not sure what else they should be doing.

"The man's back, the man's back," Jack shouted, hoping that everything would be all right again.

Janice looked up but immediately knew from Patrick's demeanour that he hadn't been successful in recovering her belongings.

"I couldn't catch the fuc...," he began before correcting himself in front of the kids, "I'm so sorry."

Janice rubbed the tears from her face.

"D'ye live nearby?" he asked.

Janice could only manage a shake of her head, the ability to speak had all but deserted her.

Her young daughter looked at the kind stranger and said, "We came by bus."

"I see. D'ye want me to call someone?" Patrick offered.

Janice gave a stifled cough which seemed to ease the pressure on her voice box. "There's no one else to call," she just about managed to say.

Patrick grimaced and scratched the side of his head although it wasn't in the least bit itchy.

"Look, I've got to go, will ye be all righ'?" he asked.

Janice put on a brave smile that wasn't fooling anyone. Patrick checked his watch and loudly exhaled. He searched his trouser pocket, retrieved a ten euro note and pressed it into the palm of the woman's trembling hand.

"It's all I've got," he said, embarrassed. He felt terrible about abandoning the young family but he had very little choice. "Ye migh' be able to get yerself a taxi or somethin'. I'm really sorry but I have to go."

Patrick sprinted along the pavement, already fifteen minutes late for work. He had to take evasive action in order to dodge an elderly walker who gave him her best discerning scowl as he raced past. He raised his arm by way of an apology but didn't waste time looking back.

Tommy Kenny, the petrol station manager, had his face twisted in an ugly sneer as he watched Patrick through the large glass window racing towards him. Kenny was a real jobs-worth who thrived on misery and never gave his staff any leeway if he could help it. Rumour had it he could peel an orange in his pocket with a boxing glove on although no one had actually witnessed the feat. Patrick finally reached the door.

"Late again, Bridges," Kenny said, tapping his smart phone, the only intelligent part of him, against his thigh and enjoying the scenario immensely.

Patrick put the brakes on and gulped in some badly needed air.

"Sorry, Tommy..." he started to explain but was immediately interrupted by the man's raised hand.

"Mr. Kenny to you," the manager said, correcting his subordinate.

"I stopped to help this poor woman, her bag got snatched and there was thousands inside," Patrick explained.

"Nice story but do I look as if I give a toss?" asked Kenny.

Patrick rubbed sweat from his forehead and said, "Ye don't understand, she only just borrowed it from a loan shark. She's desperate to get her kids outta the dump she's livin' in."

The manager gave a pitying shake of his head.

"Did you ever think of writing a book? I'd say that Hans Christian Anderson lad is shitting himself," laughed Kenny.

The Good Samaritan was seriously considering dropping his boss with a swift uppercut.

"Last warning," said Kenny, "Any excuse and you're gone. Understood?"

Patrick glared at the insensitive bastard for a moment but held his tongue. He decided the dope wasn't worth doing time for and headed towards the rear of the shop, disappearing through a door marked staff.

The locker area was that compact you could have hoovered it by standing in the hall outside and reaching in but at least it was clean. Glossy pictures of The Waltons, The Ingles and a few other loving T.V. families adorned the interior walls.

Patrick fondly remembered watching these programmes with his mother as a kid. There were also a couple of photos of some very swanky sports cars, all of which were definitely out of his price range but at least he could dream.

"Plenty of reliable people out there looking for a job," his boss called out.

Patrick couldn't help but mimic the clown.

Despite the negative start to the day Patrick busied himself in his duties. The pay was okay and the job in general wasn't too taxing but he was well aware that he was only existing in this life rather than excelling. He'd just finished filling up one of his regular's cars, the elderly woman with the electric pink hairdo and receiving a nice tip for his troubles when a flashy sports car powered onto the forecourt. It broke hard, stopping next to him, almost clipping his hip.

"Boy racers," said the elderly woman, throwing her eyes to the heavens. She gave Patrick a reassuring smile before driving off.

The boy racer was in fact an overweight bloke named Simon who's fiftieth birthday was a distant memory. The slob had a fake tan job that could easily have been sponsored by one of them crowds who regularly advertised paint for timber fences on the telly. His floral shirt was parted half-ways down exposing a rope-like gold chain that sat proudly on a cushion of chest hair resembling the contents of a burst couch. Patrick walked to the front of the car and refused to move when Simon blasted the horn. The agitated driver then raised his two hands and shook his head but Patrick still ignored him. He was drawn to the passenger who just happened to be his ex-girlfriend, Mandy. She returned his gaze but kept her expression neutral. After a brief standoff Patrick finally stepped aside allowing the car to race forward and park in the carwash area. Mandy climbed out, trying to be ladylike but looking more like a lame pony if the truth be told. She was closely followed by Simon who proceeded to grab a handful of her ass like she was a cheap piece of meat. Mandy tried to make light of it but she wasn't fooling Patrick. The two had been an item up until recently when she'd decided to end matters. She'd finally come to the realisation that the finer things in life which she so badly craved weren't going to materialise while doing a line with a fantasist who continuously spouted broken promises. Deciding that she only had another couple of years before gravity took hold of her breasts she wasn't prepared to waste anymore of her precious time trying to snare a money man. She took hold of Simon's hand and they sauntered past Patrick into the shop as if they owned the place.

"Super deluxe carwash," said Simon, swaggering up to the counter while pushing his shades back up onto his ever receding hairline.

Mandy headed for the limited magazine rack and picked up one of the glossy publications with a barely disguised disinterest. The front cover was plastered with the engorged lips of some has-been Z-list celeb trying to look twenty years younger but failing miserably.

"Any petrol?" asked the manager.

Simon shook his head and turned to his girlfriend, "Do you want something, babe."

"A latte, hun," Mandy replied.

Simon blew Mandy a kiss but she'd already renewed her magazine flicking to take any notice. His ego slightly dented, he turned back to the decidedly unimpressed manager and said, "Latte, cappuccino and a Danish."

The manager slid the carwash token across the counter just as Mandy dropped a magazine onto it.

"This as well," said Simon. He picked up the token and handed it to Mandy, "Give this to your boyfriend..."

"Ex-boyfriend," she corrected, taking the token and walking away.

Simon smirked and said, "Whatever. Tell the loser to wash it thoroughly."

Patrick was busy wiping down one of the petrol pumps when he got a feeling that he was being watched. He turned round to find Mandy standing there with a hand on her hip and the carwash token held aloft between her index finger and thumb. Without warning she tossed it to him.

"Mandy," he said, deftly catching the circular piece of plastic.

"Patrick," she replied.

"Still with yer sugar daddy I see."

"His name's Simon. Still single?"

They stared at one another for a few seconds before Mandy turned round and headed back towards the shop.

She glanced over her shoulder. "By the way, he said to tell the loser to wash it thoroughly."

Simon had just re-housed his credit card into his tanned leather wallet after paying for the various purchases when Mandy entered the shop and made a beeline for him. She planted a sloppy kiss smack bang on his lips making sure to catch Patrick's eye through the large glass window and giving him a spiteful wink for good measure.

Simon eventually broke free. "Steady on, girl. We don't want the poor guy getting a hard-on and having nowhere to stick it," he said, looking over at the pan-faced manager.

"Pathetic," Kenny mumbled under his breath.

"Simon, quick," Mandy screamed.

Patrick was standing on top of Simon's prized vehicle whistling 'If I was A Rich Man' from Fiddler On The Roof' while hosing the interior of the car through the open sunroof.

Mr. Kenny came tearing out of the shop closely followed by Mandy and her ashen-faced lover.

"Bridges," shouted the manager, "What the fuck do you think you're playing at?"

Patrick carried on with his whistling and watering unperturbed.

"Get down, I'm warning you," Kenny roared.

Simon held his chubby cheeks in his hands unable to speak while Mandy stood next to him shaking her head in utter disbelief. The manager ran over to the tap and turned it off.

"Get your stuff, Bridges, you're fired," he shouted, almost of breath.

Patrick headed straight home after being given the boot and was now sat on his bed, taking in the bleakness of his surroundings. His life was a complete and utter mess but what could he do? He'd given it his best shot and had still come up short and way short at that. 'Feck it,' he thought, 'I'm gonna sell everythin' I own and go on the lash.'

Three gold balls adorned the front of the pawn shop like a beacon of hope for the hard up and desperate. The toughened, large shop window was filled with an assortment of items that included a barely used but expensive looking drum kit, various designer handbags and an elegant walnut coloured grandfather clock that could have been a genuine contender on the Antiques Roadshow. A fluorescent sign read: The Lord may have needed a rest but we work on Sundays. Inside the premises Patrick was engaged in intensive negotiations with the wearisome looking owner. Patrick removed his prized suit from a zipped cover he'd found in a bin one time outside a formal clothing hire shop. It was perfect save for a small tear which you'd have been hard pressed to stick your mickey through. He'd plastered a bit of grey gaffer tape over the wound, making it almost as good as new. He carefully passed his suit through the narrow opening in the Plexiglass. The pawnbroker took the jacket by the shoulders and held it up for inspection. The cut was surprisingly good and the garment looked practically new. He placed it back on the counter before examining the trousers which were also in great nick. Beads of sweat formed on Patrick's forehead, the tension of trying to secure a half decent deal showing on his face.

"I'll give you thirty quid," said the pawnbroker, scratching his chin and giving a wistful look, "And I'm being more than generous at that." He knew well that his opening bid was piss poor but this was all part of the game.

"Are ye havin' a laugh here, pal?" said Patrick, taken aback by the stingy offer. He grabbed the jacket and pointed at the label which was neatly sewn onto the shiny inner lining.

The pawnbroker shrugged his shoulders, giving nothing away.

"I know fellas who make a living out of sewing on fake labels," he nonchalantly said. He had years of experience playing at this level.

"This is no knock-off. It's worth nearly five hundred yoyos. I need two at the very least," Patrick pleaded.

The pawnbroker knew he had him. He pushed his tongue against the roof of his mouth, purposely stalling. He didn't take any joy from seeing people in desperate need but he had a living to earn and overheads to meet.

"Okay. Okay. I'll give you fifty and that's the best I can do," he finally said.

"But..."

"I've a fortune tied up in stock, take it or leave it."

"Christ, yer absolutely killin' me here, pal," Patrick said as he reluctantly handed over the suit. The pawnbroker put it aside and gave his latest unsatisfied customer a ticket in the highly unlikely event that he could somehow afford to retrieve it. He then furrowed inside his trouser pocket and pulled out a sizeable roll of cash. Patrick licked his lips as the pawnbroker doled the money out onto the counter in five euro notes, presumably to make the payout look larger. The cash was immediately whipped up by Patrick. He turned to leave but stopped suddenly. The shop owner fearing the worse glided his hand towards the panic button hidden under the countertop but he'd nothing to worry about. Patrick unclasped his watch, draped it over the palm of his hand and showed it to the pawnbroker who smiled politely but shook his head. The expert didn't need to examine it closely to know that it was a replica, probably bought from some Looky Looky on the Canary Islands. At least two or three customers tried to pawn them off in his shop every week with a sharp spike occurring towards the end of summer.

"Worth a try all the same," said Patrick, smiling wryly.

The sturdy pub door was flung open allowing a series of rapid drumbeats to escape. A few seconds later a stocky doorman with a missing neck and dressed from head to toe in black jeans and a bomber jacket, manhandled Patrick from the premises. He dumped him onto his backside on the worn cobbled street with efficiency rather than violence much to the amusement of the other late night revellers. The doorman, who was the epitome of calm, retook his sentry duty at the entrance to the boozer and folded his meaty arms. Patrick rose unsteadily and feigned a charge but stopped well short of the less than impressed bouncer. A few drunk pedestrians and a gang of angry looking lads on a stag do who were dressed as purple balls egged Patrick on but he laughed it off knowing well that a good run was better than a bad stand.

"What's with the costumes?" he managed to ask the lads as he ambled away.

"We're the Grapes of Wrath," one of them shouted after him. The rest of the bunch roared and shouted their approval, no doubt having used the line many times already that evening.

'I bet Steinbeck could never have imagined a scenario like this,' thought the well-read bouncer.

The city seemed to be growing more prosperous by the month if the ever soaring buildings were anything to go by. 'It wouldn't be long before they really were scraping the sky,' thought Larry as he flattened out his newly scavenged piece of cardboard after his other one had gotten ruined in a sudden downpour. He hoped that the architects remembered to put in fire escapes having heard somewhere before that Dublin's once tallest building, Liberty Hall, hadn't got one as unbelievable as that sounded. Finding a safe and reasonably dry place was becoming a lot harder these days especially with the influx of homeless people into the capital. He knew the diligent volunteers meant well, making sure that the downtrodden were fed and clothed but competition for space also created its own problems. Street friends he'd gotten to know over the years were now too fearful to sleep at night, preferring to kip somewhere public for a few hours during the day. He liked things the way they used to be when he'd been well looked after by his charitable regulars and often wondered was there some sort of political game of football at play, trying to embarrass the powers that be into doing something meaningful for the homeless community. Maybe it was the cynic in him talking or perhaps the alcohol. The saying about 'beggars can't be choosers' popped into his head and he decided not to share his thoughts with others and to be just grateful for any assistance he received. He propped himself against the brick wall and uncapped his newly purchased bottle of red wine. Although it wasn't a reserve it would make the job of sleeping on concrete paving slabs that small bit easier. And sure hadn't he the stars for company? He had just settled himself when a partygoer staggered in his direction. Gargled lads making their way home on their own were usually good for a few shillings.

"You wouldn't have the price of a cup of tea on you, boss?" Larry politely asked.

"No," answered Patrick, carrying on his way, his hands buried deep in his pockets just like the thoughts in his head.

"God bless," said Larry, not taking it personally, having had years of practice at being rejected. And at least the chap had acknowledged him rather than passing by as if he didn't even exist.

Patrick paused, turned round and said, "No, I really don't."

"Not to worry, son, another time," Larry replied.

Patrick grunted and staggered off. He'd gone less than ten yards further along the street when he stopped in his tracks. He returned to where the old man with the pleasant disposition was having a swig of his beverage.

"Can I sit down for a minute?" asked Patrick.

"Free country," Larry replied.

"D'ye think?"

Both men smiled. Larry bum shuffled to make room on his cardboard for the drunk stranger.

Patrick nodded towards the wine and said, "A bit harsh on the aul system I'd imagine?"

Larry took another sup then wiped his mouth with his sleeve.

"Maybe, but the cholesterol's never been lower," he said, laughing. He then mumbled something incoherent before offering the bottle to Patrick who reluctantly accepted it.

"Thanks."

"Drink up, man," said Larry, "We haven't got all night." He chuckled before getting a fit of raspy coughing that took several long seconds to ease.

'What the hell,' thought Patrick, taking a generous slug of the free beverage on offer.

With the kids safely tucked away in bed Janice retreated from the bedroom and made her way towards the tiny bathroom. Glass smashing outside in the street below gave her a start which was perfectly understandable given what she had recently gone through. She forced herself to peek through the curtains and saw a gang of rowdy teenage lads hanging round a bonfire, swilling alcohol. There was a young girl of no more than sixteen with them. She looked less than steady on her feet as she was being 'playfully' pawed and pushed from one boy to another. Janice hoped for the girl's sake that someone would turn up and take her home before things escalated but she somehow doubted it. She knew from past experiences that calling the police was a pointless exercise. This was a no go area. With the curtains closed over once again Janice entered the bathroom and checked her face in the mirror. Her left eye was badly swollen while the edges of the cut underneath were red and angry. The side of her face was a mixture of yellow and purple bruising and try as she might she couldn't cover it up. She hated calling in sick, not that it was a regular occurrence but she still wasn't feeling right and had spent most of the evening being violently ill. Her boss, true to form, was his usual ungrateful self and informed her that he wasn't paying for her absence. She closed the lid on the toilet bowl and sat down. How was she going to repay her loan to that parasite Harris? And how was she ever going to get out of this shithole? She bowed her head, gripped her hair tightly in her hands and began to sob as quietly as she could.

Patrick attempted to get to his feet but fell backwards, wedging himself against the wall in a half upright position. Larry looked up and smiled then glugged down another mouthful of the cold numbing wine.

"And I'm gonna put the gun to his head and say, your money or your life!" Patrick slurred as he made a pitiful attempt to lift his hand up and turn it into an imaginary pistol.

"Don't be a thick, you'll get ten years for that," Larry said, warning the younger man.

His companion slowly slid the rest of the way down to the ground without trying to resist.

"But ye wanna see the roll of notes the pawnbroker had," he said.

Larry belched loudly and gave his chest a couple of light taps for relief.

"Still a pittance for the risk you're taking," he warned.

Patrick gently nodded his head while conceding the older man's point.

"Yer righ', yer righ' of course," he said.

"Do you know the telly?" said Larry.

Patrick furrowed his brow as if this was some sort of trick question. "I've heard of the device," he then replied in what he believed to be a Victorian type of accent.

"Well not the actual telly itself, smartarse but what's on it, in it, you know what I flippin' mean," said Larry.

"Go on, will ye," Patrick said, almost losing the will to live.

"There's that show on it, the one with the balls?"

"Match of the Day?" asked Patrick.

Larry threw his eyes to heaven.

"Jaysus, I don't know," said the younger man, a bit miffed.

"You know it, of course you do," Larry said, racking his brain for the title. "Everyone does it, you can win millions."

"Ye mean the Lotto?" said Patrick.

Larry excitedly clicked his fingers except they didn't quite click.

"That's it. The Lotto. Now if I wanted money that badly..." he began.

The younger man wearily shook his head. "I tried it. Can't afford anymore tickets," he replied.

"Feck paying for it. Why don't you just borrow one of the machines and play it for free until you win," Larry said, giving his companion a conspiratorial wink.

Patrick stared at the crazy old man who had suddenly burst into laughter but he didn't join in. A seed had just been sown. This was an ingenious idea and a possible solution to all of his financial woes. He attempted to get to his feet so he could immediately act upon the plan but he may as well have being trying to climb Mount Everest in a pair of roller skates.

"A pen, I need a pen to write this..." he started to say but never got to finish his sentence, having slipped into a warm, fuzzy sleep, dreaming of untold riches.

Chapter 4

Monday.

A spectacularly bright dawn was making its presence felt all across the sleeping city, giving hope to a brand new day. Bottles rattled as the milkman shoved a crate of empties further towards the back of the open wagon. The door to Flynn's Mini-Mart opened and the owner appeared, bright eyed and bushy tailed.

"Morning, Frank," Mick said.

"Do you ever sleep?" asked the milkman.

Mick scratched his beard and said, "Can't afford to. The joys of being self-employed."

"I never thought I'd see the day when we'd be back using these things again," Frank said, referring to the glass bottles.

"That's them hipsters for you. Won't drink milk from a plastic carton anymore and want to save the world while they're at it," said the shopkeeper, not at all convinced by the Green party's manifesto.

Frank deposited a fresh crate into Mick's arms.

"It's made my day twice as long, that's all I bleeding know," he said.

Mick smiled. "How's the wife by the way?" he asked.

"Off sunning her arse in Spain no less, while I burst me hole here in this kip," the milkman replied, "Oh and she only wants a teak conservatory when she gets back."

"Timber? In this country?" said Mick, knowing well that he was only adding fuel to the fire.

The milkman screwed up his face and his eyes seemed to grow closer in his head.

"Isn't that what I said but she was having none of it. Some influencer posted a photo online and now the wife's convinced that her life won't be worth living unless she gets one too," He climbed back into his electric truck, tooted the clown-like horn and was on his not so merry way, disturbing the rest of the neighbourhood with his rattling crates of planet saving bottles.

"Ahh," shouted Patrick as his leg kicked out of its own accord, his muscles going into a spasm and knocking over several empty wine bottles. When his jittery leg finally relaxed he glanced round. Larry, his new drinking buddy, was curled up in a foetal position, snoring loudly. He sat up slowly, his head all groggy and began to massage his stiff neck, gradually bringing it back to life. Sleeping rough on a concrete footpath was no bed of roses. He had a banging headache and could fully empathise with Bob Geldof and The Rats' dislike of this particularly day of the week. A nagging thought came to the fore, something about the Lotto. His addled brain was grinding through the gears not quite clicking and then he remembered. Larry's ingenious idea of stealing, no, borrowing a lottery machine and playing it for free. A passerby dropped a ten euro note at his feet as they strode past without missing a step. Unsure of what to do at first, Patrick cautiously picked up the money and stared at it as if he had never seen a paper note before. Maybe this was an omen, a sign of future wealth? Whatever it meant he got to his feet and dusted himself down. He contemplated waking his partner in crime to split the windfall but decided to leave the man sleep, he'd no doubt bump into him again soon enough and would sort him out. With a renewed spring in his step he headed off down the street to realise his destiny.

Some whining Country and Western tune escaped from the backroom of Flynn's Mini-Mart where Mick was making tea.

"Is it one or two sugars again?" he called out to Tina who was leaning over the shop counter, lazily flicking through a fashion magazine.

"Just the one, have to watch the figure," she shouted in return while subconsciously smoothing the pocket on the rear of her spray painted jeans.

Mick spied through the slightly ajar door leading into the shop, leering at his unsuspecting employee's pert bottom. He put his index finger in his mouth and sucked on it then stuck it into Tina's tea, giving it a quick stir. When the heat became too much for him to bear he shoved his finger back into his mouth and sucked on it once again.

"Don't worry, love, I'm watching it for you," he whispered, his face twisted in a lustful grin.

Patrick marched into the shop feeling like a man of importance with his newly acquired ten euro note safely tucked into his trouser pocket. He went straight to the shelves where the newspapers were on show and picked one up.

"Is that tea ready yet, I'm gasping?" Tina called aloud.

Patrick turned round and gave the shop assistant a quizzical look but she just gawked back at him as if to say 'what's your problem?'

"Coming," shouted Mick from the backroom.

Patrick went to the counter and set his paper down. He then subconsciously began to examine the lotto machine which was positioned to one side. Too busy to notice that he was being watched by the shop worker, he stooped slightly trying to check underneath the machine. He then placed his hands on both sides and tried to move it but it was firmly fixed in place.

The customer was getting on Tina's wick.

"Did you lose something?" she asked impatiently.

Patrick glanced up at her, his train of thought momentarily disrupted.

"Here you go, darling," Mick said, arriving with the freshly brewed tea and placing it next to Patrick's newspaper. The shopkeeper nodded towards the tabloid's headline and said, "That bloke was lucky he had the cash."

Patrick had been so engrossed with the lottery machine that he hadn't taken much notice of the paper until then.

"*Kidnapper Frees Man After Substantial Payoff,*" he quietly read to himself. He looked out through the store window into the distance and said, "Wasn't he just."

Tina sneaked a look at her boss, crossed her eyes and twirled her finger next to the side of her head. The owner did his best not to laugh and mouthed 'stop' but without anger.

"I see the lotto wasn't won again," Mick said, trying to change the subject.

"Is there anything else?" asked Tina, loudly enough to get Patrick's attention.

The customer turned back to face her.

"Yeah, a quick pick for the main draw," he said, handing over his tenner.

"That'll be a jackpot of at least six million on Wednesday I suppose," Mick said, "If I won it I might just take Tina here off on a staff holiday, she deserves a big bonus." He laughed at his own innuendo and headed for the backroom.

"In your dreams," replied Tina, knowing too well what her boss was insinuating but he'd have to come up with a lot more than a holiday if he fancied tasting some of her sugar.

Patrick snapped up his paper and printed lotto slip and left without saying another word.

"Your change..." Tina called after him but he was already gone.

"Christ," yelled Mick. He'd just given himself a nasty scald on his forearm with the kettle, letting it crash to the ground. He should have been paying more attention to what he was doing but he was already imagining rubbing baby oil onto Tina's naked body, the next employee of the month winner.

Patrick had dashed home from his shopping trip and wasted no time packing, hastily shoving bits and pieces into a sports bag which had never once been used for such activities. He had taken it with him on a few occasions while sauntering through his local park of a Saturday morning, convinced that it made him look kind of cool and that he somehow fitted in with the other sports enthusiasts. Fresh socks and underwear were flung into the bag, enough to keep him going until he achieved his objective. He dragged his bed away from the wall leaving enough space to get in behind. He dropped to his knees and managed to lift up a loose floorboard on the third attempt of asking. There, hidden underneath in a mass of cobwebs was a silver Smith and Wesson handgun. A random thought popped into his head. He remembered his Da telling him that farmers would sometimes use cobwebs to stem the bleeding when dehorning young cattle. It gave him nightmares at the time but he'd never looked into it to see if it was true although knowing his dad it probably was. He gave the handgun a quick wipe then tucked it into his waistband at the base of his spine just like he'd seen in countless American gangster movies and television shows. This was so exciting and he couldn't believe that he hadn't thought of robbing a lottery machine himself. He'd have to buy aul Larry a case or two of wine. Quality stuff though and not that other mank shite he was used to knocking back. He picked up the container of fish food from the windowsill and tapped some powdered flakes into the sparse bowl where his solitary goldfish appeared to be held in suspended animation.

"I'll be back in a few days so just kick back and relax," he told his pet.

Jaws gave a swift kick of his fantail and motored towards the surface where he began to gobble up everything in sight. Patrick hesitated before chucking in the rest of the grub.

"Don't eat it all in one go, I'm warnin' ye," he said. "Try and pace yerself, bud." He then turned to his Venus flytrap. "As for you, Mallet Head, yer just goin' to have to fend for yerself and use those jungle instincts of yers."

Satisfied, he scooped up his packed sports bag and headed for the door.

"Nearly feckin' forget," he said, tapping himself on the side of the head with his knuckles. He hurried to a shelf next to his single bed and selected a CD from his very limited collection. Written in gold against a black background was the appropriately named album, ABBA GOLD. He began to sing, "Money, Money, Money," as he left his flat in search of great riches.

Girlish laughter could be heard coming from flat 1B. Patrick was stood outside, staring at the door. He checked his watch, it was just after midday so he presumed they were long since up. He gave a polite knock, nothing too loud but hopefully enough that the young couple would hear. He waited patiently and was about to knock again when the door swung open. Tommy appeared, his bare-chest gleaming in sweat and with a tool belt hanging round his tidy waist over his blue jeans. Patrick caught a glimpse of Tommy's partner, Debbie, in the background wearing little more than what looked like a flimsy piece of pink fluff and a naughty smile. He immediately averted his eyes.

"Sorry for disturbin' ye," he said.

"Yer grand," replied Tommy, somewhat out of breath, "I was only helpin' the missus with a bit of DIY."

"Righ'," said Patrick, not picking up on the innuendo. "It's just that I'm going away for a few days to try and patch things up with herself," he lied, "Wondered if ye would mind keepin' an eye on me place for me?"

"No prob," said Tommy.

"Not that there's anythin' worth robbin'," Patrick added.

Tommy laughed kindly and said, "I know the story only too well. Anywhere nice?"

"Eh... somewhere ye can shop, it's her favourite pastime," answered Patrick. It suddenly dawned on him that he'd been so caught up in his own world that he actually hadn't a clue what Mandy really liked to do with her free time.

"Where's my handyman gone?" Debbie called out from deep within the room.

Tommy nodded his head, winked and said, "I hope she's not expectin' me to use the tradesman's entrance."

Mick was busy doing a stock check of his ice-cream goods when Patrick entered the shop to carry out his plan of 'borrowing' a lotto machine. The place was dead quiet. Patrick scuttled behind the tin foods section trying to work up the courage but finding the whole thing very stressful.

Mick thought he'd heard a customer enter and glanced in Patrick's direction forcing him to quickly duck down. Patrick held his breath.

"Better get more choc-ices," Mick muttered to himself already losing interest and resuming his stock taking.

Patrick eyeballed the produce on the shelf next to him and selected a tin of Bachelor's baked beans, gripping it firmly in his sweating hand. Weighing approximately four hundred and twenty grams, the humble can of beans didn't appear to be a very deadly weapon. That was unless you decided to bring it crashing down on some poor sod's head of course! What was the optimum speed and level of aggression needed to knock a person out but without actually killing them or inflicting serious brain damage? This was the dilemma now facing Patrick as he edged closer to the proprietor of Flynn's Mini-Mart. He hovered over the shopkeeper who had his face stuck in the large chest fridge decorated with colourful stickers advertising the delicious ice-creams within. Mick was oblivious to the peril he now faced. Patrick stared at the weighty can of beans in his outstretched hand which seemed to be getting heavier by the second. It was now or never! He raised the tin high above his head almost touching the fluorescent lighting before quickly bringing it earthward bound towards the shopkeeper's skull. At the very last moment however he just about managed to stop himself short. 'What the hell was he thinking of? This wasn't who he really was. And how in the name of Jaysus had things come to this?'

"Can I help you with something?" Mick asked, his face still stuck in the fridge.

The question startled Patrick. He immediately dropped the beans and bolted for the door before he could be identified. The shopkeeper lifted his head and was puzzled to see the unidentified customer fleeing. Annoyed, he straightened up and marched towards the exit in pursuit of the culprit.

"What do you think you're playing ahhh..." he began to call out but didn't notice the abandoned can until it was too late. He stood on the tin and his foot ran away from him sending him flying hopelessly into the air. Time seemed to stand still as the shopkeeper's arms and legs flailed in all directions like some astronaut mucking about in zero gravity or a zany cartoon character attempting to defy gravity. His descent to earth however was rapid and he landed with a bang, walloping his head off of the chequered tiled floor.

The shop door slowly closed behind Patrick leaving him standing outside on the pavement wondering what he should do next. Conflicted, he finally turned round and headed back inside to apologise only to discover the shopkeeper lying prone on the floor, out for the count. Acting on impulse, Patrick hurriedly locked the front door, flipped the sign round to 'closed' and pulled the cord on the venetian blinds. His shallow breathing was now the only sound to be heard in an otherwise eerily quiet room. He slowly scanned the place and spotted the now slightly dented can of discarded beans loitering close by, feigning innocence. He bent down and picked it up. Although he knew he shouldn't, he was more than a little amused at the situation.

"It's not what we do, it's the way that we do it," he softly said, referencing the famous duo, Barney and Beanie's tagline on the label. If he didn't know better it also appeared as if they were laughing back at him, sharing the joke. He rubbed his chin with his free hand and glanced over at the Lotto machine, the sole reason he had come here in the first place. 'It could be you,' he thought, gently shaking his head while remembering the advert used in the United Kingdom where a giant index finger would pick out random people. 'And why not him?' he thought, hoping that the lottery would finally be the answer to all of his financial woes.

Chapter 5

Mick blinked his eyes rapidly, trying to focus on his surroundings. It quickly became evident that he was in his flat above the shop. A sharp pain shot up through his spine as he attempted to move forward causing him to immediately freeze. Although the back of his head was throbbing furiously, that was the least of his worries right now. His mouth was taped shut and both his arms and legs were tied tightly with blue nylon rope to a chair. His memory was fuzzy. One minute he was counting the ice-creams in the fridge and someone had come into the shop and then... Alerted by footsteps climbing the stairs, he turned his head gingerly towards the open doorway and held his breath in trepidation. Seconds later Patrick appeared, wearing ladies tights over his head. He could see the fear flickering in Mick's eyes.

"Now I don't want to have to hurt ye, pal," Patrick said, moving towards his prisoner. He'd watched enough television in his time to know that you had to assert yourself from the get-go. He crouched down and rested on one knee as if he was genuflecting.

"I'm gonna remove the adhesive tape but don't get any ideas or start shoutin' like an aul wan or else I'll be forced to use this," he warned in a commanding, no nonsense tone. He produced the handgun which was tucked into his waistband at the rear of his pants and pointed it at his victim. Mick squeezed his eyes shut, terrified.

Patrick was somewhat taken aback by the shopkeeper's reaction and felt a tad guilty.

"Relax, will ye," he said, changing tact and trying to put his prisoner at ease.

Mick reluctantly opened one eye at first and then the other. His captor placed the gun on the floor and paused momentarily as if giving himself some time to think. He then leaned forward and attempted to catch the corner of the tape which was covering the shopkeeper's mouth. Patrick's clammy hands were noticeably shaking making it near impossible to grip the tape properly. He rubbed them briskly along his jeans doing his best to dry them before making another attempt. This time he had a lot more success. The sticky tape was ripped clean off along with a sizeable amount of the prisoner's facial hair.

"Ahh," roared Mick.

Patrick was startled. He grabbed his gun and jumped to his feet, fearing that the entire neighbourhood would have heard his prisoner's roar. He spun round towards the door about to do a runner but accidentally pistol whipped Mick in the process. The shopkeeper was knocked backwards and sent crashing to the floor while still tied to the chair. Patrick looked down at his upended victim who was clearly in a lot of pain. He ran his hand over his head, made a few steps towards the door but reluctantly returned.

"I told ye to be quite. Look wha' yer after makin' me do," he said by way of an apology. A small amount of blood trickled from Mick's bulbous nose and his cheek was already beginning to swell.

"My moustache you fecking moron. You're nearly after tearing the damn thing off," shouted the unimpressed shopkeeper.

Patrick raised the palm of his hand and said, "Shush, shush. I'm sorry."

"Imbecile," muttered Mick.

Patrick bent down and grabbed hold of his prisoner and the chair and with a great deal of effort just about managed to right the pair of them. He took a step back, caressing the base of his spine and said, "I think I'm after pullin' a bleedin' muscle." He massaged his back some more, pulling all sorts of faces as the shopkeeper looked on incredulously.

"If I was a bad fecker, and this is just how mad this country's gone," Patrick said, wagging a finger at his prisoner, "I could sue you for damagin' me back. But of course I'd never be that petty and it's not wha' I'm here for."

Mick was seething with this smartass stranger's intrusion into his life but was doing his damndest not to escalate things.

"Just take what you want, I won't cause you any trouble," he said.

"Sorry again," Patrick apologised.

The shopkeeper didn't want to hear any more apologies. "What are you after?" he asked.

Patrick gave a child-like smile and said, "I need to borrow yer Lotto machine for a day or two."

The machine was tipping along nicely, printing off one crisp, quick-pick ticket after another. With the ladies tights disguise long since discarded Patrick sat on a high stool behind the counter, his legs crossed at the knee and a lit cigarette in hand. He was doing one of those puzzles in the newspaper where you had to make up as many words as you possibly could from a larger word but he was seriously struggling. He glanced across the page to check the minimum recommended score. Thirty-six words for adults and twenty-two for children. He totted up his own score and discovered that he had only managed to find twelve. And of that total, two of them were complete guesses and one was a rude word which he didn't think would be allowed. 'Them kids must have no bleedin' life,' he was thinking to himself when the machine suddenly stopped printing the lotto slips.

A message flashed up on the screen - *Please Sign Off.* He banged his fist hard on the counter. This wasn't on. He was on a schedule and had a deadline to meet. He took the stairs to the upstairs flat two at a time and stormed through the door but was immediately stopped dead in his tracks. Mick was slumped in the chair, his head tilted fully forward and his chin squashed against his chest. At first there wasn't a sound. And then Patrick heard it. Snoring. The fecker was in the land of nod.

"Wake up," he shouted.

The shopkeeper's eyes shot open as he wobbled in his chair having absolutely no idea where he was.

"That bleedin' machine of yours is after stoppin'," Patrick roared.

"What time is..." Mick said through a half suppressed yawn but stopped abruptly. He spotted that his kidnapper was no longer wearing his nylon disguise.

Patrick ran his fingers through his hair, completely frustrated. He never imagined that such a simple task like borrowing a lotto machine would prove to be so stressful. It was then that he realised he'd left the tights on the counter below. He instinctively raised his hand to cover his face but it was too late. Way too late.

"Shite," was the only thing he could manage to utter.

Mick squeezed his eyes tightly shut.

"I didn't see anything," he pleaded, "I swear. Not a thing."

His captor slowly removed his hand from his face, resigned to the fact that his identity was now known. He blew out loudly expelling all the air he'd stored behind his cheeks, taking a moment out to think.

"It won't matter in anyway," he eventually said.

"Ah Christ, you're going to kill me now, aren't you?" Mick said, almost crying but with his eyes still firmly shut.

"Wha'?" said Patrick, a little confused. He then copped onto what the shopkeeper was implying. "No, shut up will ye and don't be so dramatic," he said, He took another moment to gather his thoughts. "Why were ye on about the time?" he then asked.

"The time?" Mick said, trying to remember what he'd said. It suddenly came back to him. "Oh, the time. Yeah, all the machines shut..."

"Open yer flippin' eyes will ye, it's makin' it very hard for me to concentrate," said his captor.

Mick reluctantly did as he was told but made sure to only look down at the floor.

"The machines need to shut down so they can update the software. They'll be live again in the morning," he explained.

This wasn't the kind of news that Patrick wanted to hear. He paced back and forth across the still room, his mind churning through the gears and the various scenarios it was throwing up. Mick watched him out of the corner of his eye, hoping that the lunatic would come to his senses and end this madness. Patrick stopped and scratched his chin.

"So the machines go back on in the mornin'?" he asked.

Mick gave a hesitant nod.

"Nothin' more we can do so until then," Patrick said, "Better go back to sleep for yerself."

Before Mick had the chance to utter a single word in protest Patrick grabbed the tape from the sideboard and plastered his gob.

"Nigh', nigh'!" he said and left the room, closing the door after him.

Tuesday.

The deserted street was silent except for Frank the milkman depositing his early morning deliveries onto the pavement outside Flynn's Mini Mart. Surprised not to bump into the shopkeeper he looked up at the closed bedroom curtains with mounting curiosity.

"Strange that," he said, climbing back onto his electric vehicle to continue on with his rounds. Whatever was going on with the shop owner was none of his business and he'd still get paid once he made the deliveries. It was up to his customers to cancel things; he'd enough on his plate as it was, especially trying to find the money for his wife's new teak glasshouse.

The rattling bottles from the milk float outside woke Patrick from his pleasant slumber. Although he was still dressed in his clothes he had a far better sleep than the previous night under the stars with only a scrawny piece of cardboard for a mattress. He checked his watch then jumped out of bed. "Things won't get done of their own accord," he declared.

The main shop door opened slowly and Patrick's head tentatively appeared. He spied the deliveries outside on the pavement then did a swift check up and down the street. Happy that the coast was clear he whipped in the goods and shut the door again. Hopefully he wouldn't be here too long as he hated the thought of good food going to waste, a remnant from his impoverished childhood days no doubt. He was sure that he'd read somewhere that the great actor and comedian, Charlie Chaplin had felt the exact same way.

With the deliveries stacked away at the back of the premises it was time for Patrick to sort out something for the breakfast. He picked up a basket and took a stroll down the refrigeration aisle. This was the life. The essentials were popped into the basket; rashers, sausages, black and white pudding, mushrooms and of course a tin of baked beans. A batch loaf, a block of real creamy Irish butter, none of that cholesterol busting imitation gick and a box of eggs completed the fare. He gave his chin a good rub and decided that his stubble needed attention. A razor blade set and shaving foam were placed in the almost overflowing basket along with a new toothbrush and toothpaste. He had standards to maintain after all.

"Ye can keep yer internet, this is wha' home shoppin' is all about," he cheerfully said.

The kitchen was a mess with used pots and pans scattered all over the place but Patrick didn't care. He would give the entire place a good cleaning later on but satisfying his hunger took precedence right now. Delighted with his culinary skills, he loaded the freshly made fry-up onto two preheated plates. The grub along with two mugs of piping hot tea, milk, sugar and enough toast to feed a small army were all placed onto a long tray.

"Lovely, jubbly," he said, sniffing the mouth watering aroma wafting from the fry-ups.

Patrick gently pushed open the door with the toe of his shoe, whistling a cheerful theme tune from a television programme whose title he couldn't quite remember. Smacked in the face by an awful stench, he almost dropped the breakfast. He managed to gather himself and deposited the tray on the sideboard. His sweatshirt was quickly pulled up over his nose and mouth to act as some sort of buffer from the foul smell emanating from the lifeless prisoner. He stood for a moment before deciding to edge closer, fearing the worst.

"Christ, wha' have I done!" he said. It was never his intention to kill the chap, just to put the frighteners on him temporarily until he could achieve his goal. Images of being banged up with some hairy overweight bloke who was mad for late night cuddles suddenly flashed before him.

Mick's eyes shot open causing Patrick to stumble backwards. He held his chest while trying to calm his breathing as the shopkeeper glared back at him like a rabid dog. And then it dawned on Patrick.

"Ah Jaysus, are ye after havin' an accident?" he asked.

Mick was not in the least bit impressed.

"Why didn't ye give me a shout or somethin'?" added Patrick.

The shopkeeper rocked back and forth in his chair, mumbling angrily. Patrick then pointed at his prisoner's taped mouth.

"Oh yeah, sorry," he said. He slowly removed the tape conscious this time of Mick's remaining patchy, facial hair.

"I'll fucking kill you when I get free, I swear," the shopkeeper screamed.

Patrick was taken aback by the outburst. What was this guy's problem? He tapped his handgun which was tucked into the side of his jeans to remind Mick who was in charge. It had the desired effect.

"We all need to take a step back from the edge here, pal," Patrick calmly said. "Could ye not have held it?"

Mick's initial anger was morphing into mortification.

"I'm very regular," he said.

"I see," replied Patrick.

"I usually go around nine every night," the prisoner reluctantly revealed.

"Well ye've another thing comin' if ye think I'm washin' and changin' ye," Patrick said with a little giggle, trying to make light of the awkward situation. He immediately stopped once he realised that Mick wasn't enjoying the joke and was in fact sobbing. Actually sobbing and the real mad shoulder jerking stuff into the bargain.

"Ah Janey Mac, will ye stop that," Patrick said kindly, finding the situation quite disconcerting. He bit down on his lower lip trying to give himself time to think.

"Look, we'll sort somethin' out, don't be worryin'," he said.

Mick's sobbing gradually subsided and was replaced by the occasional sniffle instead. Patrick removed a clean handkerchief from his pocket and held it up to the shopkeeper's nose.

"Give a few aul blows and ye'll be grand," he advised.

The shopkeeper did as he was told and blew hard. Patrick carefully removed the contaminated handkerchief with his finger and thumb, making sure to hold it as far away as possible. He then flung it into the empty fireplace.

"I don't know wha' ye were cryin' about in anyway, ye've just ruined me poxy breakfast," Patrick said with a smile.

"You're going to tell everyone, aren't you?" said the shopkeeper.

"About wha'?"

"You know?"

"Doin' the business in yer cacks?"

Mick refused to answer.

Patrick grinned and said, "Of course I won't. I'll tell ye somethin' for nothin'. Ye don't see this kind of carryon in any of them hostage movies, do ye?" He grimaced, trying to work out what to do next. "It could be worse," he said.

Mick shot his captor an incredulous look.

"Don't be givin' me the hairy eyeball," Patrick warned, "Anyway, where was I?" He glanced up at the ceiling for inspiration, "Ah yeah, it could be worse. I overheard a taxi bloke in a pub one time tellin' his mates about a fare he'd picked up goin' to the train station. Yer man was some big mouthy politician," He clicked his fingers trying to recall the name, "Does be always on the telly constantly sproutin' numbers to back up his lies?"

The shopkeeper wore a blank expression much to Patrick's annoyance.

"Yer no bleedin' help," he said, "He's a mad head of curls and an eye that twitches like a car indicator."

Mick shook his head not sure how much more of this madness he could take.

Patrick threw his hands in the air in defeat. "Doesn't matter. So the taxi is headin' towards Heuston station and the driver gets this wicked smell. Yer politician man was only after gickin' himself." Patrick left out a cheeky laugh. "As ye can imagine the driver was havin' none of it and starts roarin' and threatenin' to fuck yer man into the Liffey. He said the politician bloke had his head in his hands, was in bits from the gargle and pleaded with the driver to stop the shoutin'. He said he'd pay for the cab to be cleaned. The driver told him he'd be payin' for the loss of earnings too plus a few extra quid to keep schtum. The politician thinkin' he was back in the Dail bar with the other Hooray Henrys starts to get a bit uppity, tellin' the taxi man he won't be blackmailed and threatenin' to go to the guards."

The shopkeeper wasn't in the least bit interested in Patrick's nonsensical story but it wasn't as if he could go anywhere and he just had to sit there and suck it up.

"The driver was made of sterner stuff however and let yer man know that unless the reddies were forthcomin' every taxi-man across the city would have the story within the hour with the rest of the country in the loop by the time the Angelus hit its first bong. Anyhow, a deal was done to cover the fare, the cost of the cleanup, the loss of earnings and most importantly the hush money. The taxi chap was also given cash to run into a shop on the way to the station to pick up a new pair of jeans. The politician hurried onto the waiting train clutchin' his new jeans but not before callin' the taxi-man a thievin' Jackeen bastard. Apparently the politician made a beeline for the toilets onboard and locked himself inside so he could get cleaned up. A few minutes later after the train had pulled out of the station the politician flung his dirty trousers and underpants out the window and into a mass of brambles. When he removed the jeans from the bag he discovered that the taxi fella had only gone and bought him a jean jacket instead."

The shopkeeper allowed himself a little smile having absolutely no love for government officials who seemed to pass laws on a whim which he then had to pay dearly for.

"The story goes that the politician geezer hid in the toilet for the remainder of the journey until he was eventually forced to pull the emergency cord to get the ticket inspector's attention. He ended up getting off the train wearin' an oily CIE overalls," Patrick explained.

Mick was going to point out that the taxi-man couldn't possibly have known what happened to the politician after he'd exited the cab but hey, why let the truth get in the way of a good story.

"What about sorting me out?" he asked instead.

"No bother and we'll organise somethin' so that it doesn't happen again. Alrigh'?" Patrick said, trying to reassure his prisoner.

Patrick ripped a cornflakes box in half and then proceeded to carefully write a message on it in big black marker. *Due To A Family Illness The Shop Will Remain Closed Until Further Notice. Sorry for the hassle, Mick.* He parted the blinds and popped the sign into the window. "That's another little job out of the way," he said, clapping his hands loudly and congratulating himself. He returned to the lotto machine, readying himself for a tough day at the office. The machine had other ideas however. *Please Sign In And Enter The Code.*

"For the love of Jaysus," he sighed, holding both sides of his face, "Why do they have to make everythin' so bleedin' complicated." He lowered his hands and took a couple of deep breaths. "Keep calm, everything's under control."

Mick was wide awake, lashed and bound to his chair. He knew what was coming next when the goofball downstairs discovered that he needed a code to print more tickets. He turned his head towards the door in anticipation. The stairs began to creak.

"He's shagged now, isn't he," the shopkeeper chuckled to himself, "And I'm telling him absolutely nothing. Spend another night trussed up like a cooked fucking chicken, I don't think so."

The door swung open and Patrick appeared, his head tilted to one side and wearing a sinister smile. Mick's bravado vanished in an instance. His captor strode towards him and pulled back the tape but it didn't hurt as much this time. Patrick had earlier taken the time to shave off a circular area from around Mick's mouth to prevent a repeat of the previous misunderstanding. The prisoner immediately rattled off the code without being asked. Patrick fixed the tape back in place and left the room without needing to utter a single word. Mick let out a long sigh through his nostrils, relieved for small mercies but also ashamed at his cowardice.

Boredom was kicking in as Patrick listened to the mind-numbing printing actions coming from the lotto machine as it dutifully got on with its job. There were a few novels on one of the racks but he wasn't a big reader even though his mother had done her best to get him into it with the Ladybird book series. The small little boxes in some of the tabloids with their quirky stories were about as much as his limited attention span would allow. Maybe he'd give it another go when he won the lottery and was sunning himself by the pool at his luxury villa. A bit of music was just what he needed right now. He strolled into the backroom and popped open the CD slot on the stereo but was dismayed to find an album titled *The Best Country & Western Music Collection Ever #2*. The thought that there was a part one knocking about somewhere made it even worse.

"Some people have absolutely no taste," he said, immediately binning the offensive material. He nipped upstairs and retrieved a CD of his own from his sports bag. Back downstairs again he banged on his favourite album, ABBA GOLD.

"Can't beat a bit of Scandinavian bliss," he said. He repeatedly hit the fast forward button until he reached track number 9 and then pressed play. Piano music instantly filled the stagnant air. The tempo increased and then the magical lyrics of Money, Money, Money began.

"La la la la, la la la la,

La la la la la la la la,

La la la.

Patrick hummed the opening lines even though he had the words off by heart. He sashayed his way from the backroom into the shop, continuing to hum along.

"La la la la la la la

A poxy shillin' left for me..."

The packed bus eased to a halt opposite Flynn's Mini-Mart.

"I'll collect you about six then, love?" the chunky driver said, giving Tina his best cheesy smile as she alighted from the vehicle.

"The only way you'll be picking me up, sonny, is if you're still working, otherwise take a ticket and join the queue," Tina replied with a cheeky wink, taking absolutely no offence to the chancer's chat up line.

The driver gave a hearty laugh and drove off. Having the banter with someone who wasn't easily offended and who was able to give it back in spades always made his day go quicker. Another passenger, a woman in her early thirties, who had also gotten off at the same stop turned to Tina.

"Why do I never get an offer like that?" she asked, her face lit up in a pleasant if not sad smile.

Tina looked her up and down and shook her head slowly.

"Don't take this the wrong way now, princess," she said, "But it you got rid of that tash waving at me, split your uni-brow in two and maybe lost a couple of stone things might change."

The woman was appalled. She stood there, her mouth opening and closing like a freshly caught fish floundering in a boat. Tina didn't mind giving anyone a bit of advice but she wasn't a miracle worker. The woman's eyes were now opening and closing in tandem with her lips as her brain struggled to comprehend what she'd just heard.

"Are you still there?" Tina said, arching a perfectly shaped, tinted eyebrow.

"Cow," was the only thing that the mortified woman was able to blurt out by way of a response. She spun round and briskly began to walk away.

Not one to be outdone, Tina of course had to have the last word.

"At least I have tits big enough to be milked," she called out. "I see they're auditioning for the new Star Wars film, you'd be perfect for the role of that big hairy yoke, Two Backas."

The woman almost fell over as she scarpered down the street trying to put as much distance as possible between her and the deranged woman. The rain which had been forecast finally arrived in the form of a misty drizzle. Tina put her umbrella up to protect her newly acquired hairdo and crossed the street not in the least bit put out by the unsavoury encounter. She was confident that if things had escalated she would have had no bother taking your woman out with a few well aimed slaps.

Patrick was caught up in his singing and had no idea of the impending disaster with Tina now only yards away outside. He'd snapped the head off of a mop and was using it as a wig while the broken handle had become his microphone.

"La la la la la la la,

I'm gonna find me a wealthy woman.

La la la la and have a ball

La la la la.....

Outside, Tina was searching through her handbag for the shop keys while also trying to balance her umbrella.

"Loads a bleedin' money,

La la la la,

La la la la..."

She eventually found her keys nestling at the bottom of her bag but not before almost catching one of her freshly fitted false nails into the bargain. The key was inserted into the lock and she leaned down on the handle. As Patrick twirled round the floor he somehow noticed out of the corner of his eye the door handle moving. He froze but only for a split second before dropping his 'mic' and flinging off the mop wig. He then raced to the stereo, belted the stop button and held his breath. The door remained closed with the handle held in the downward position. Aghast, he spotted that the safety bolt hadn't been pulled across. A heavy goods vehicle trundled by, rattling the large shop window which momentarily distracted Tina.

"Ah, there ye are, love," greeted Janice, from under her own brolly, having just arrived.

Tina pursed her botox filled lips but said nothing.

"Didn't realise ye were on as well this mornin'," added Janice.

Tina wriggled the key about in the lock.

"Yeah," she said, trying her best to concentrate on undoing the lock, "Mick needed time off, had to go into town on business and he wasn't sure whether you'd show up this morning."

The comment irked Janice but she said nothing.

Patrick ducked low and scurried towards the door, sliding the bolt across just as Tina attempted to push it open. The door wouldn't budge so she leaned into it and gave it a good shove.

"Bleedin' brutal weather we're havin', isn't it?" Janice said, trying to put the previous comment from her mind as she looked up at the cloudy sky which seemed to be growing darker by the second.

Tina continued her struggle with the door but without much success.

"Havin' problems?" Janice asked.

Tina looked up and said, "Seems to be jammed..." Her expression changed in an instant, "What in the name of Christ happened to your face?" she asked, more than a little alarmed.

"Ah, it was me own fault, tripped over the rug in the sittin' room," Janice softly replied while absently raising a hand to caress her face. Try as she might, she couldn't conceal the bruising with any amount of makeup. "Should've been payin' more attention." She didn't want to make a fuss and she definitely didn't want to talk about her business with Frank Harris or the scumbag who mugged her. It was then that she noticed the sign in the window and pointed to it, grateful for the distraction.

"Did ye see this?" she asked.

Her colleague followed her finger and read the note.

"I wonder who's sick?" Tina said. "Don't remember Mick mentioning anyone."

"Jaysus. I hope they're alrigh' for his sake," said Janice.

Tina's five seconds of sympathy were all used up and she said, "Yeah, whatever."

Janice looked perplexed. "That's a bit odd though, don't ye think?" she said.

"What is?" asked Tina.

"The wording," Janice said, gently tapping the glass at the second sentence. "In all the years I've worked for Mick I've never once heard him use that phrase, 'Sorry for the hassle'."

"Who knows, maybe he's started doing crystal meth," Tina bluntly replied. "Anyway, it's still poor communication. I mean, how am I supposed to manage this place when I don't know what the fuck's going on from one day to the next?" She immediately noticed her colleague's horrified expression. "Oh, I thought you knew, love. Mick made me the manager yesterday when you were off but don't you worry, things won't change that much."

Janice couldn't believe her ears. Her whole world was tumbling down around her and no matter which way she turned she just couldn't catch a break.

"Look, I'll give him a buzz, see what's happening," Tina said. She didn't show it but she was absolutely seething inside. When she got hold of Mick she was going to give him an ear bashing, putting her in an awkward position like this.

Sitting on the floor with his back firmly pressed against the other side of the door was a mightily relieved man. Patrick blessed himself, more out of habit than belief, that he'd been able to slide the bolt across in the nick of time. A fraction of a second later and he was rightly foooked. As he was beginning to relax and get his heartbeat down to something resembling normal a mobile phone started to ring. He quickly scanned the room. The noise was coming from under the fridge. He quickly crawled over on all fours, retrieved the phone and hit cancel.

Outside, Tina held her mobile to her ear and gently shook her head.

"No joy," she said. "Might as well go home, I'll try him again later and will let you know the score."

Chapter 6

It was early evening in the flat above Flynn's Mini-Mart and Patrick was relaxing in a comfy armchair, tucking into a freshly made chicken curry. His reluctant companion was struggling to eat his dinner due to his rope constraints. He was tied to the chair with one arm fixed behind his back and with just about enough slack to feed himself with his other hand.

"Look, you know that you can't possibly get away with this," Mick said through a mouthful of surprisingly tasty rice.

Patrick rested his fork on the side of his plate and looked at his prisoner, waiting to hear more.

"The odds are stacked against you even if you did the eight thousand euro worth that this shop usually sells."

Patrick bit down on his lower lip and exhaled noisily through his nose.

"You can't just keep printing tickets, you know," continued Mick, oblivious to Patrick's darkening mood. "The lotto people monitor the machines for any major irregularities in the playing patterns and if they find any they immediately contact the shop in question."

Patrick gripped the side of his plate, his knuckles growing white.

Mick began to laugh and said, "And let's just say that if by some complete and utter fluke that you actually won the jackpot you'd need me, the shopkeeper, to help you with your claim."

A few grains of rice escaped from Mick's smirking mouth but were quickly gathered up by his roving tongue in a lizard-like fashion.

"You see, I get a bonus for selling the winning ticket," he continued, laughing all the while, "So you can't possibly get away with it."

The plate narrowly missed his head as it went whizzing by, smashing against the wall behind and spraying him with curried rice. Patrick jumped from his chair, overturned it and gave it a few kicks for good measure. He then snatched Mick's plate and forcefully threw it to the floor, stamping all over the mess. The shopkeeper was flabbergasted by the man's violent actions.

"I've got ten thousand in the safe below, just take it and go," he blurted out in the hope that things wouldn't escalate even further.

Patrick gripped his hair in his hands and shouted, "Ten grand! Ten measly grand!"

The shopkeeper tried to make himself look as small as possible as he sank back into his chair. Patrick balled his hands into fists and stomped around the room watched closely by his prisoner. He stopped dead in his tracks and jabbed a finger in Mick's direction.

"D'ye not understand?" he said, almost crying, "I want millions. I need millions."

The doors of several presses in the backroom of the shop were reefed open as Patrick hastily searched through them.

He found a cardboard box stuffed with various masks and colourful Halloween costumes while a vacuum cleaner and dusting equipment were shoved to one side. His search finally paid dividends when he came across a metal toolbox. He opened it and found exactly what he was looking for. There, glistening in the box was a claw hammer with a polished head and a slick hickory handle. He picked it up and held it in one hand before transferring it to the other, getting a sense of the weight. Not too heavy but solid enough to do the job even if it took a few extra wallops. He stood up and gave a swift practice swing to get a real feel. Satisfied, he began to rhythmically tap the metal head against the palm of his hand while staring up at the ceiling and grinning wildly.

Loud banging echoed throughout the still building. In the upstairs flat, Patrick raised the hammer and belted it against a screwdriver which was acting as chisel. It punched a hole through the seat of a wooden kitchen chair, an exact replica of the one his prisoner was tied to. Mick watched with dread as his captor worked away, a sheen of sweat glistening on his forehead. When Patrick was happy that he'd completed his task, he took a step back to admire his handiwork. The kitchen chair now possessed a crudely cut circle bang in the centre. He wasn't going to make a master craftsman with the City of Guilds anytime soon but it was still perfect for what he had in mind. He glanced over at Mick and smiled.

"That should sort ye out in case ye get caught short again," he said, business like, "But ye migh' want to be careful of the aul splinters."

Mick frowned as it eventually dawned on him what the man's intentions were. No more accidents!

"Oh yeah, nearly forgot," Patrick added. He turned and abruptly left the room.

The shopkeeper looked forlornly at the chiselled out chair. What did he do to deserve this? He must have been an awful bastard in a previous life. Patrick returned moments later with a plastic bucket and a red sleeveless dress. He set the bucket down under the hole in the chair before holding up the dress.

"I would have never imagined red as yer colour, considerin' yer skin tone like," he joked.

Mick was flustered.

"Don't be so ridiculous, that's my ex's," he said, defending his manly reputation.

"Whatever. Ye don't need to explain yerself to me and sure anyway, I think that people in general should be more understanding and acceptin'," Patrick honestly replied.

"Don't tar me with that shagging rainbow brush," the shopkeeper said, unable to disguise his contempt.

Patrick shrugged his shoulders and said, "Whatever floats yer boat. Ye better get changed outta them clothes, there's a bad smell in here."

The lotto machine dutifully churned out more quick-pick tickets as Patrick counted a large bundle sitting on top of the counter. 'It had been a long day but nothing worth doing comes easy,' thought Patrick. The clock struck nine p.m. He glanced up at the ceiling, put his index finger into his mouth against the inside of his cheek and immediately flicked it back out again making a 'Plop' sound. He smiled before returning to important paperwork of his own.

Chapter 7

Wednesday.

The day of the draw had arrived at last. Patrick lay on top of the bed, casually blowing smoke into the air. He listened to the excited chirping of the sparrows outside as if they knew what was going to happen. Once he'd won the lotto he could begin his new life in earnest. He'd be able to buy whatever he wanted, whenever he wanted and there'd be no shortage of girls queuing up to date him. He hopped out of the comfy bed and pulled the curtains wide open. The room was immediately filled with glorious warm sunshine. He stretched his arms fully towards the ceiling before bringing them slowly back to his sides in a gentle, half circular motion while taking in a deep breath and exhaling slowly. He'd once seem some sham doing similar stretching exercises in the park in order to relieve stress and thought it was worth a go even though he'd had one of his best sleeps in years.

Things were a little bit different in the neighbouring room however where Mick was gagged and bound to the uncomfortable wooden chair, vacuum packed into a dress several sizes too small. He was slumped forward, moaning in his sleep. Every so often his head would jerk violently upright when the pressure on his airways increased as his chin sunk deeper into his bulky chest. After a few short moments his head would loll to one side and slowly sink downwards until the whole process was repeated once again.

"Not quite breakfast in bed I know but a very close second none the less," Patrick announced as he entered the living-room carrying a tray laden with an array of appetising food. Mick didn't reply as he was still in the land of nod or at least teetering on the edge of it. Patrick sat the tray down on the table and took a step back to admire his hard work. Not only had he cooked up enough sausages, rashers, eggs etc. to feed a small army, he'd also found a plastic rose and had used an empty coke bottle as a vase to complete the look.

"Wakey, wakey, sleepy head," he said in what he imagined to be a maternal sort of voice. There was no response. He gave the leg of Mick's chair a gentle kick.

His prisoner began to stir, the aroma from the freshly made fry wafting up through his nostrils. Patrick pulled his sweatshirt up over his mouth and nose and bent down to retrieve the bucket from under the shopkeeper's chair.

"Thank Jaysus this is the last day of sloppin' out, wha'?" he said but in a jovial manner.

Mick took no notice of the comment. He slowly rotated his head one way then the other, trying to stretch out his deeply knotted neck muscles. He'd definitely have to pay a visit to his favourite masseuse down near the quay to get some relief. The parlour used an Oriental wellbeing clinic as a front for its seedy activities and was a very popular place judging by the footfall. He felt himself grow hard just at the thought of it all. Patrick carried the bucket away at arm's length and left it outside the stale room. He would sort it out later. The windows were then opened wide to allow in some badly needed fresh air. Happy now, he took his jumper away from his face.

"Did ye a special treat seems how it's gonna be our last breakfast together," he cheerfully said, carefully removing the tape from the shopkeeper's mouth. "French toast as well as the usual."

"I'm speechless," Mick sarcastically replied.

Patrick ignored the less than appreciative remark and rigged the shopkeeper up as before so he could tuck into the grub while it was still hot.

"Meant to ask ye earlier, wha' happened to yer hand?" he said through a mouthful of food.

"I scalded it," replied Mick, struggling to manoeuvre his fork towards his gob.

"Nasty," his captor said with genuine sympathy. He pointed his fork at Mick's dress and said, "I have to tell ye, the red's growin' on me."

The shopkeeper ignored the smart arsed comment, instead trying to concentrate on eating as quickly as possible. Although he'd been doing nothing these past few days apart from sitting on his backside he was absolutely ravenous.

"I've decided that when I win the jackpot tonight yer gonna help me to collect it and we'll split it fifty-fifty, fair's fair," Patrick said.

Mick began to choke on a piece of pudding. His face grew alarmingly purple while his eyes seemed to almost bulge out of his head as they rapidly filled with water. Patrick dropped his fork onto his plate and scrambled over to his prisoner. He made a fist and walloped the shopkeeper several times across the back until the piece of food was dislodged and sent flying across the table. Mick gulped in some life saving air before sucking up a mouthful of tea through a straw. Although Patrick didn't show it he was mightily relieved. He sat back down and resumed his breakfast, trying to play it cool.

"For all yer airs and graces yer table manners leave an awful lot to be desired, d'ye know that?" he said.

Mick glared at him through blurry eyes. He was contemplating the payback he was going to dole out once he got free when his mobile phone rang.

"Does that thing ever stop," asked Patrick, nodding towards the shelf over the mantelpiece where he'd left it.

Mick didn't bother to reply. Patrick reluctantly got to his feet and checked the caller I.D. but didn't answer it.

"Yer wan's persistent, I'll give her that," he said.

To say Tina was vexed that Mick wasn't picking up her calls was a massive understatement. She was absolutely livid.

"Where the fucking hell are you?" she shouted, losing count of the times she had now called. Enough was enough. She was going to go round to the shop and give her boss a piece of her mind.

The breakfast dishes had been scraped clean and stacked in the sink to soak in the sudsy water. Patrick would wash them later but he'd more important tasks to be getting on with in the meantime. He pulled off a fresh piece of tape for Mick's mouth.

"You wouldn't do me a massive favour, would you?" the shopkeeper sheepishly asked having recovered from his earlier near death experience.

Patrick looked puzzled and gave a casual shrug of his shoulders.

"If I can?" he said.

Mick gave a polite cough. "It's just that I do the same lotto numbers every week..."

Patrick laughed kindly as he sealed his captive's mouth. "And ye want me to do them for ye?"

Mick nodded.

"No problem but if ye win I'll have to bleedin' kill ye," laughed Patrick.

With a bit of ABBA's Fernando in the background chilling things, Patrick was sat on the shop counter relaxing with his legs dangling, child-like. A freshly brewed mug of tea rested next to him as he used a fifty cent coin to leisurely scrape away at a scratch card. There was a small pile of used cards lying on the counter next to him. None of them had yielded any money so far, only the offer of another free go. He wouldn't normally bother with them as he thought the odds of winning were ridiculous but each to their own. In the background, the lotto machine continued to spew out more quick-pick tickets.

"You wouldn't reach up there my good man and pass me several more of those scratch cards?" Patrick said to himself in an ever so posh voice.

"Certainly, bud," he replied in his own Dublin accent. He ripped off a fresh strip of cards hanging overhead and lobbed them onto the counter.

"You're too kind," thanked the posh speaking Patrick oblivious to the two elderly women who were standing outside the shop, reading the sign in the window. The disgruntled shoppers shook their heads and waddled off down the street, dragging their two-wheeled trolleys behind them, grumbling a string of complaints as they went.

The expensive car pulled up outside the neglected Georgian House which was barely held together in places by the numerous coats of paint it had been smothered in over the years. Patrick's landlord was fed up waiting for rent he knew from experience would never be forthcoming. He brought backup with him this time in the event of trouble. A solid framed man with broad shoulders and a fraction over six-two stepped out of the vehicle causing the suspension to breathe a sigh of relief. He was the landlord's brother, detective Murphy. The landlord also got out of the car but his movements were a lot less efficient due to his lard arse and pregnant belly. Detective Murphy gave his brother a scornful look which the landlord pretended not to witness. He shuffled round to the rear of the vehicle, popped open the boot and retrieved his toolbox and a roll of heavy duty refuse sacks.

This was a no nonsense visit and detective Murphy wasted no time in planting his foot against the door lock of Bedsit 2A and bursting it open. It was obvious that he had plenty of practice in this department.

He turned to his brother and said, "This is the only language these scumbags understand."

The landlord gave a compliant nod and the pair immediately got to work.

The landlord and his brother were only minutes into their eviction duties when Tommy from the downstairs bedsit came storming into the room after hearing all the commotion.

"Wha' d'ye think yis are bleedin' doin' in here?" Tommy shouted.

The landlord had been busy stuffing his absent tenant's clothing into the black bin bags and glanced over at his brother for reassurance. Detective Murphy knew that his sibling hadn't the stomach for confrontation and took a step forward. His expression was a mixture of pity and disdain as he sized Tommy up.

"I'm evicting the little parasite," the landlord said, feeling a lot braver with his older brother now positioned between him and his angry tenant.

Tommy was having none of it. He fancied his chances with these two, knowing that the fat one was all mouth and would shit himself if he dropped the stockier bloke first. The only problem though, was that he'd end up homeless and trying to get another place, even an awful kip like this was almost impossible. He couldn't do that to his partner.

"Ye can't just break in," he said, "I'm callin' the law."

Detective Murphy approached Tommy with a controlled arrogance, reached into his inside pocket and produced his thick, tanned leather wallet. He flicked it open with a practised ease and flashed his I.D.

"There's no need, I'm already here," he smugly said.

The landlord smirked and thought, 'The first chance I get I'm going to raise that upstart's rent and we'll see how he likes it.'

Murphy put an arm round Tommy's shoulder and escorted him outside the room with just the right amount of pressure.

"So you can run along now knowing that everything's under control and we'll all remain the best of friends," he said. He winked at Tommy then shut the door in the younger man's face. He turned round to where his grinning brother was busily tearing down the beautiful poster of the Amazon Rainforest from the wall.

"What's next?" asked the detective.

The landlord scouted the room. Almost everything had been bagged.

"The stuff on the window-ledge has to go as well," he said.

Murphy strolled over to the ledge, picked up a pair of reading glasses and promptly snapped them in half without giving it a second thought.

"What do you want me to do with the goldfish?" he asked.

"Dump it," said the landlord not giving a toss that it was a living creature.

The detective nodded and said, "Smelly poxy things in anyway." He picked the fishbowl up and emptied the entire contents, including Jaws, down the toilet. "Enjoy the ride," he said then flushed.

Drilling echoed throughout the tired building. Detective Murphy climbed the groaning stairs which were protesting madly under his considerable bulk. He'd just finished dumping the last of Patrick's belongings into an industrial sized wheelie bin at the rear of the property. The place was a shithole and he could never imagine living in a kip like it.

"That's the last of the rubbish," he told his brother who was on his knees securing the last screw into a brand new sturdy padlock.

"Perfect," the landlord said, struggling to get to his feet. "I'm all done and dusted here too. I can only imagine the waster's face when he returns."

Detective Murphy smirked and said, "It's a pity I didn't get to meet him in person all the same."

Although the day had dragged, Patrick wasn't in the least bit disheartened. All of his hard work these last few days was finally going to come to fruition and tonight he was going to be a lotto multi-millionaire. He sat nestled in the comfy armchair, sipping tea and watching the television. Across the room Mick was tied to his chair, staring curiously at the enormous pile of printed lotto slips heaped up on the table. The National Lotto music began and the presenter appeared on screen with his usual cheesy grin, dressed in a double breasted suit that might have once looked fashionable.

Mick nodded towards the tickets. "If you don't mind me saying, how on earth are you going to check them all?" he asked.

"What's that?" Patrick said, glued to the box.

"The lotto slips, how are you going to check them?" the shopkeeper repeated.

Patrick turned his head towards his prisoner and smiled.

"Easy-peasy. As soon as the draw's over I'll bang on their Twitter page and wait until they confirm it's a Dublin winner..." He turned his attention back to the t.v. "And then, individually I suppose."

On screen the numbered balls were released into the spinning drum and sent twirling into a bouncing, hypnotic frenzy. This part always reminded Patrick of the Demolition Derbies he'd joyfully watched as a kid whenever he was allowed to. Some of the foster parents he'd lived with thought that it only encouraged violence and banned it. Undeterred, he'd always found a way to sneak a look. The lotto balls were sucked up like an alien spaceship abducting cattle from a field before being spat back out again and rolling into place.

"Five, fifteen, nine, twenty-two, eight, twenty-one and the bonus number thirty-two," the presenter gleefully announced. "Thanks for playing sensibly and the very best of luck."

Patrick used the remote to switch the television over to the Twitter page. The time in the top corner of the screen read 8pm.

"Did you not bother to do the Euro millions while you were at it?" the shopkeeper asked sarcastically.

Patrick furrowed his brow while slowly shaking his head. "Are ye mad?" he replied.

'Well there's the kettle calling the pot black,' Mick thought but decided to keep the saying to himself.

"Didn't want to attract too much attention, bud," said Patrick as if it was the most obvious thing in the world. "Can ye imagine the hassle tryin' to stay anonymous with that sort of a jackpot? Besides, ye'd run the risk of bein' kidnapped just like that woman's nephew down the country." He clicked his fingers several times hoping that it would spark his memory. "Doris or somethin' along those lines."

"I believe her name was Deloris," said Mick.

"That's her. Anyway, I heard it's costin' her an absolute fortune in security."

"But I've already been kidnapped," Mick said.

Patrick looked sceptically at the shopkeeper. "Ye were? By who?" he asked.

Mick cocked his head and it took a few moments for the penny to drop with his captor.

"G'wan outta that," laughed Patrick. "This is a totally different scenario. It's more like a business arrangement and ye just needed a friendly shove in the righ' direction, that's all."

Mick shook his head in disbelief.

"You'll be thankin' me later on, ye'll see," Patrick said, rubbing his hands childishly together, "When we're both rollin' around in the big money."

The shopkeeper wasn't sure if he was expected to respond to this ludicrous suggestion so he decided to give a gentle nod of the head.

"In the meantime it's best to just sit back and relax," Patrick advised before taking a satisfying sip from his mug of tea. He was starting to believe that the planets were finally aligning nicely in the universe, not that he was big into the aul horoscope craic but you just never knew.

'Easy for you to say,' thought Mick as he shifted uncomfortably in his hard wooden chair. He was really beginning to fear for his safety when the screwball didn't win the jackpot.

Bleary-eyed, Patrick finished taking a leak and gave his hands a good rinse. He could hear his late mother reminding him to wash them properly especially between the fingers where the dirty maggoty germs lurked. He looked at his reflection in a bathroom mirror that wasn't much bigger than a postage stamp and barely recognised who he saw. His eyes were bloodshot and he seemed to have aged considerably which was ridiculous of course given the fact that he'd only been here a few days. He splashed cold water onto his face and relished the soothing effect. As soon as he won the jackpot he promised himself that he'd get a bit of work done, nothing too radical mind, just a little nip and tuck here and there. If it was good enough for movie stars and millionaires then it was definitely good enough for him. On the other hand, he didn't want to end up looking like your man with the Irish sounding name he could never remember. He was a ruggedly handsome chap until he'd destroyed himself with one surgery too many. On second thoughts, maybe a facial would be enough along with a few jumbo drums of Oil of Olay or Ulay or whatever it was called these days.

The Twitter feed on the television screen had been updated. There was no winner of the lotto in Dublin let alone anywhere else in the rest of Ireland for that matter. Mick was visibly trembling at the thoughts of what was going to happen next. His captor appeared innocent, even simple at times and that worried him even more. A bona fide criminal would more than likely have smacked him around a few times when he'd first taken over the shop but this nut hadn't laid a finger on him apart from the mishap with the gun at the beginning. Christ, he'd even been apologetic at times. Whistling distracted Mick from the television. He immediately recognised the tune as ABBA's Money, Money, Money. Patrick strolled into the room and knew from the shopkeeper's expression that something was up. He followed his prisoner's line of sight and spotted the 'No Winner' tweet. The whistling immediately ceased. Mick found himself straining against his restraints in a futile attempt to break free even though he had severely tested them in vain countless times over the last number of days.

Patrick took a deep breath before exhaling loudly.

"If at first ye don't succeed then try and try and try again," he said in a surprisingly upbeat kind of way.

That was it. The shopkeeper had enough. His nerves were unravelling faster than a Catherine wheel on bonfire night.

"Would you ever get a life you bleeding fruitcake," he screamed, "You're not going to win the lotto, not now, not ever. Take the ten thousand euro I have in the safe and fuck off back to whatever nuthouse you managed to escape from."

Silence filled the room for what seemed like an eternity when in reality it was only a matter of seconds. Patrick rested his hands on his hips, the epitome of calm.

"Well, if yer finally finished ye big drama queen. I'm gonna win, it's my destiny," he said. He pulled up a chair in front of the mouthpiece and sat down. Mick instinctively recoiled. Patrick removed the gun from his waistband, primed the chamber and pointed it squarely at his prisoner's forehead. The shopkeeper squeezed his eyes shut as if this would somehow protect him from being shot. He'd seriously underestimated the sort of man he was dealing with.

"And another thing," Patrick calmly continued, "If you ever disrespect me by raisin' yer voice again like that I'm gonna have to put a bullet in yer loaf of bread."

Things went quiet again. Mick didn't want to witness his own death but the curiosity was getting the better of him. He cautiously opened one eye at first and then believing that he'd been given a reprieve, he opened the second.

"Look, I'm sorry about the outburst just now but can't you see that this plan of yours is going absolutely nowhere," he said, tentatively.

Patrick arched an eyebrow before lowering the gun to his side. This was definitely not how he envisaged things going and he was seriously regretting ever initiating the plan.

"The draw is over and the odds of you winning were staggering," Mick cautiously continued, "And if it's of any small consolation I think the idea was extremely clever. Maybe if you had a bigger syndicate, who knows. Anyway, there's no real harm done so I won't report you to the authorities if you just up and leave right this minute."

Patrick grinned but held his tongue.

"Besides, you can't do the draw for Saturday unless..." Mick immediately shut his trap but it was too late. He'd already said too much.

Patrick shot forward in his chair and pounced on the slip up.

"Go on, unless?" he said.

The shopkeeper refused to answer and tried to avert his eyes from his inquisitor. Patrick began to drum his fingers rhythmically on the kitchen table.

"I don't like to be kept waitin'," he said coolly but the threat was explicit.

Realising that he'd well and truly put his foot in it, Mick had little choice but to spill the beans so to speak.

"It's just that there has to be sufficient funds in your account for the direct debit to go through. If not, you won't be allowed to take part in the next draw and could even end up losing your licence," he revealed.

Patrick joyfully clapped his hands together and sat back in his chair pondering his next move. "Excellent," he eventually said, "So where's this ten grand ye keep tellin' me to take?"

Chapter 8

Thursday.

The hot shower had invigorated Patrick and he was rearing to go once again. With his bedsit keys in hand he eased open the door of the upstairs flat a few inches and peeked his head round. Mick was still bound to the chair, sound asleep. Satisfied, Patrick gently closed the door and left his prisoner to his dreams, hoping that they were pleasant ones. It was time to return home and check in on Jaws and Mallet Head and to pick up some clean jocks and fresh socks for his extended stay.

Patrick took the granite steps up to the looming Georgian house two at a time, happy to be getting a break from the intense business of hostage taking. The once grand building had slowly fallen into its current dilapidated state but nobody seemed to give a toss, not least the owner. Patrick's steps rang throughout the stairwell area giving off an eerie feeling as he slowly made his ascent. He knew he was in arrears with the rent and that his grumpy landlord's patience was wearing thin but that would all be rectified as soon as the lotto scheme paid dividends. Sure he'd even give him a few quid extra just to show that there were no hard feelings between them.

The sparse room which Patrick called home was unrecognisable. He stood in the middle, looking round in complete shock not believing that his landlord would have actually followed through with his threats of eviction. 'The landlord's hero must have been that sham, Cromwell,' he thought. With all of his belongings gone he was extremely surprised to see the empty fishbowl still intact on the windowsill. He picked it up and held it aloft, mourning the loss of his innocent friend, Jaws and trying not to imagine how he'd met his untimely end. A gentle knock at the door took him from his morbid thoughts. He turned round to find his glum-faced neighbour, Tommy, standing awkwardly, not knowing what to do with his hands. He finally decided to shove them into his jean pockets just to get them out of the way.

"I tried to stop them..." he said, his sentence trailing off.

Patrick gave a slight nod, "Righ'."

"He had a copper with him," Tommy explained.

"Probably his brother, he's a dick," answered Patrick, remembering the landlord's threat from his previous visit.

"Ye can say that again," said the neighbour.

Patrick smiled. "No, I mean he's a detective. Works out of Store Street, I think."

"An arrogant fucker wherever he's based," Tommy replied, not bothering to disguise his contempt.

Patrick gently placed the fishbowl back on the windowsill and rubbed his chin, contemplating his next move.

Tommy shifted his feet slightly and said, "Yer stuff's in my place. I took it outta the wheelie bin as soon as they'd gone."

"And Jaws?" Patrick excitedly asked, hoping against hope.

Tommy wore a blank expression.

"Me goldfish?" said Patrick.

"Didn't see him, bud, sorry."

"Sound. Ye couldn't give me a minute?"

"No prob. Call down whenever yer ready, we're not goin' anywhere," Tommy said before leaving.

Patrick rolled his tongue round the inside of his parched mouth trying to moisten it even a small bit. He was also doing his best not to shed a tear for his poor fish in case the floodgates really opened up. Wandering aimlessly about the bedsit he couldn't help but think back to the good times they'd had together, even when that stupid plastic clam thing had closed unexpectedly, catching a piece of his tail fin and trapping him inside for what felt like an eternity. When the shellfish eventually released Jaws Patrick had reefed it form the jar and dropkicked it across the room. He'd then spent the next hour or thereabouts staring into the jar, making sure that his pet was moving okay. He went into the bathroom to take a leak and almost leapt with the fright. Swimming in the toilet bowl was none other than his prized fish.

"Jaws," he shouted with the kind of unbridled joy usually reserved for people welcoming home their loved ones at the airport having not seen them in years.

The couple living in the flat beneath Patrick's stood humbly at their door while smiling awkwardly at their neighbour. Debbie linked her boyfriend's bare arm while her head rested against his solid chest. She was extremely proud of the way her man had stood up to that bully of a landlord and his less than law abiding brother. The fact that Patrick was so far in arrears never entered the equation. Tightly held under Patrick's arm was the fishbowl containing a very energetic goldfish who was no doubt relieved to have been rescued from the toilet bowl.

"Oh yeah, nearly forgot," said Tommy, taking a pair of glasses from his shirt pocket and handing them over to the other man.

Patrick threw a puzzled eye over the spectacles which were held together with white insulating tape.

"They were in the bin with the rest of yer stuff. I patched them up as best I could," Tommy said, "I wish we could have done the same for yer telly."

"The bollix," Patrick swore then quickly looked at Debbie, "Sorry for the language."

"Yer alrigh'," said Debbie, "I'm well used to it living with this big galumph." She gave her fella a playful thump in the upper arm.

Her partner pulled away, feigning injury but then smiled.

"I woulda used black tape if I had any," he said.

Patrick removed his glasses and checked them over. "They're grand, thanks again. Righ', I better head…"

"Yer sure ye have a place to stay?" Tommy asked.

"Positive," said Patrick, careful not to reveal where he was actually holed up.

"We've plenty of room and the couch is always there until ye get yerself sorted," Debbie offered.

"Thanks, that's very kind of ye," said Patrick, feeling humbled. "And I know ye have loads of room as well as a tradesman's entrance."

Debbie shot Tommy a slightly confused look but he just shrugged it off.

"I'll be back in a coupla days for me things, not that I've much stuff to collect," he added.

She gave Patrick's arm a consoling rub and said, "No worries, love. It's not as if we'll be goin' away on holidays anytime soon."

Patrick had decided not to wallow in things once he'd returned to the shop following his eviction. If anything, it was the kick up the backside he badly needed to refocus his sights on the sort of lifestyle he craved and what he needed to do to achieve this objective. Rattling bottles outside on the street grabbed his attention and he couldn't help but sneak a look through a corner of the off white net curtains. The dust nearly gave him an asthmatic attack and he had to pinch the bridge of his nose to suppress a sneeze. Stood below was the milkman, reading the sign which Patrick had previously stuck inside the window. The milkman suddenly looked up and Patrick had to duck back quick smart so as not to be seen. He held his breath for a few moments. His nose was rearing itchy and he was doing his best not to sneeze. The milkman scratched the thinning hair on his head then disappeared out of sight, down the side passage.

"Where does he think he's goin', the nosey fecker? And how many times does he have to read that note before he gets the bleedin' message?" Patrick said, praying that the deliveryman would just sling his hook.

After a few seconds the milkman came back into view and returned to his vehicle, pulling a face that only a mother could love.

"Finally," said Patrick.

Everything nowadays was Google this and Google that but not for Patrick. He was definitely old school when it came to the latest phones and apps and all that palaver. Playing game consoles was one thing but they could keep all this online crap to themselves. He'd watched numerous documentaries and read plenty of newspaper articles warning people of the dangers of giving up their anonymity to an all powerful digital being. No, the old fashioned Yellow Pages would do just fine he decided as he leafed through the physical sheets of paper. After a quick search he found what he was looking for and promptly punched in the number on his outdated, pay as you go mobile or his Blockia as he liked to refer to it. The call was answered almost immediately by a refined gentleman's voice.

"Howaya, pal... Yeah, I'm good, thanks," Patrick replied in a genial manner. He'd put the disappointment of not winning the previous nights lottery far behind him and was mad for action once again. "I want the executive genuine calfskin briefcase with the Brinks coded lockin' system and it better not be that imitation shite from China." He popped open the till revealing a drawer full of notes. Despite all the talk about the massive increase in the use of bank cards it was clear that in this locality cash was still definitely king. The man on the phone said something but Patrick was too busy visualising how smart and professional looking he was going to be, throwing shapes with his expensive new case by his side.

"D'ye deliver?" he asked… "Well, that's a bit inconvenient to be honest." He scratched his chin giving himself time to think. "Tell ye wha'," he said, "Courier it over, I'll cover the cost and there's a twenty spot in it for ye as a tip, can't say fairer than that."

With the few essential jobs out of the way it was time for grub.

"They say that the most important meal of the day is the breakfast," Patrick said, scoffing another tasty, crispy coated sausage sandwich.

"Do they?" Mick replied with as much enthusiasm as having to go to the debs with your sister 'cause nobody else would take her.

"Well I firmly disagree," continued Patrick, not one to be deterred by his prisoner's lacklustre response. "The most important meal of the day is definitely the one yer eatin' because there's no guarantee ye'll be getting' another one." He pointed his fork at Mick. "So count yerself lucky, pal that I'm such a kind and thoughtful chap."

The shopkeeper forced a smile. His attention was drawn to the expensive new briefcase still in the clear plastic wrapper sitting on the sideboard.

"By the way," Patrick said, nodding towards the goldfish which was swimming around in its modified bowl. "Mick, meet Jaws. Jaws, meet Mick."

Boredom could be a killer when you were holding someone hostage but not in Patrick's case. He was a man with a plan. "I O U," he said aloud as he wrote on a piece of paper, "Fifty-euros, thanks." He added the slip of paper to several others already in the till which still contained a sizeable but dwindling amount of cash. He slid the till closed and got to his knees. He rolled back a rubber floor mat exposing a section of tiles which was slightly darker than the surrounding area. Methodically, he began to tap each one of the ceramic squares in turn with the end of a screwdriver until he heard the hollow sound that he was listening for. "Presto," he said. He stuck the flat end of the screwdriver between the joint in the tile where there was an absence of grout and easily whipped it up, revealing a safe underneath. He opened it without any fuss and retrieved a cloth bag. The draw strings on the bag were released and he stuck his hand inside taking out a bundle of cash. He held it aloft for a moment, his eyes growing as big as saucers before giving it a kiss.

The city hummed as people went about with their daily lives, hustling past one another, eager to get to their various destinations. A couple of bystanders bucked the trend as they blocked the footpath, gawking through the window of the pawnbroker's shop. A middle aged woman giggled to herself while an older man next to her shook his head as if to say 'I've seen it all now.' Inside the shop, Patrick had stripped down to his boxers, holding the new briefcase by his side, waiting patiently as the proprietor retrieved his suit from a rack. The owner was more than a little surprised when Patrick had rocked up with the cash presuming that he'd never see him again. After the pawnbrokers, a trip to one of the many sex shops which seemed to be popping their heads up all over the city soon followed. Sturdy handcuffs were acquired from the saleswoman who assured Patrick with a wicked grin that they were good enough to restrain any size gimp. He wasn't sure what she was on about and politely declined her offer to 'give them a go,' telling her that he'd pressing business that needed sorting.

He cut a dashing figure as he strut his stuff along the street, dressed in his tailored suit with the briefcase securely handcuffed to his wrist. The area had changed and he barely recognised it now with all the fancy apartments guarded behind tall, ornate railings and watched over by numerous, less than discreet cameras mounted on poles. Where once there were worn council owned flats bursting with the rhymes and laughter of children from lower income families now stood lonely, sterile and overpriced apartments. "That crazy communist chap was right after all," Patrick whispered to himself as he remembered his neighbours' sceptical attitudes back in the day.

A van boasting the latest technological advances in close circuit television was parked on the edge of the footpath directly outside the period building which housed the bank. Patrick entered but not before holding the door open for a grateful elderly woman, allowing her to exit. He kind of wished he was wearing a trilby like the movie stars from the forties and fifties just so he could tip it. The smell of money seemed to seep out through the walls of the bank even though a lot of stuff was now done electronically. Patrick licked his lips as he watched one of the tellers, a well groomed young man, expertly counting out a sizeable bundle of notes. Although the queue flowed steadily it still wasn't moving fast enough for Patrick. He ran a finger along the inside of his shirt collar, scratching an itch that wasn't there before flicking away the tiny droplets of perspiration which had formed on his upper lip.

"Next," the bank teller called out from his cubicle prison.

Patrick didn't hear the instruction and was startled when the man behind him in the queue tapped him on the shoulder. He instinctively reefed his briefcase backwards and took a defensive stance fearing an attack but preparing to strike if he had to. The man smirked then nodded towards the free teller. It took Patrick a split second to realise what was going on. He rolled his shoulders and slowly rotated his neck, trying desperately to appear casual. Swaying up to the counter, he couldn't help but glance back. The man in the queue was staring at him. Patrick put two fingers up to his eyes and then pointed them at the bloke indicating that he was someone not to be messed with. When the briefcase was unceremoniously slammed onto the counter the young bank worker behind the protective glass gave a little jump. Patrick made a big show of wiggling the handcuffs before opening the case.

"Can't be too careful," he said, looking back again at the man in the queue and giving him the evil eye.

The bemused teller smiled but kept his gob firmly shut. He'd thought he'd seen it all in his short stint at the bank but obviously not. Even the CCTV specialist at the top of the step ladder who was repairing a dismantled camera did a double-take.

The earlier cloud cover had all but dissipated leaving a sunnier, more refreshing day in its place. The weather seemed to mirror how Patrick felt as he emerged from the bank and the bounce was definitely back in his step. He sauntered along the street, whistling aloud before coming to a halt outside a newsagent where a familiar Lotto sign protruded proudly from the shop wall. He decided to pop in and do a quick pick despite the fact that he was printing tons of them for free back at Mick's. Old habits were hard to beat. Within minutes he emerged from the premises folding his newly purchased ticket in half and slipped it into his shirt breast pocket, content with the world.

'Just as well I changed out of me good suit,' Patrick thought, judging by the amount of fresh cream and jam that was stuck to his hands. On his way back from the bank he'd also picked up a few fresh doughnuts from a small bakery he knew well as a little treat for the tea. And if he thought he was messy Mick was in a worse state altogether with his face smeared with the gorgeous gooey filling from the buns. In fairness, the rope restraints didn't help his prisoner much.

Patrick smacked his lips tightly, savouring the last of the sugary particles.

"That hit the aul spot, wha'?" he said as he gathered up the used packaging and began to tidy things away.

"You can say that again," Mick agreed, "I wonder how many Weight Watcher points its cost me though?"

Patrick accidentally knocked over the milk carton spilling the contents over his jeans.

"Shite. Have ye a washin' machine in this gaff?" he asked, stepping back from the mess.

"Press, downstairs backroom," answered the shopkeeper.

"Sound. Wha' were ye sayin', yer on a diet or somethin'?"

"Sort of," Mick replied.

Patrick paused his tidying, raised an eyebrow and said, "I have to be honest with ye, pal and I'm not tryin' to be mean here but ye'd never have guessed."

"You could always lie, it's great for ones' self esteem," the other man answered, pretending to be offended.

"It's all a load of bull in anyway, these diets. The basic problem is yer arsehole isn't as big as yer mouth."

"Thanks."

Patrick shook his head, smiled and said, "Not just yers, everyone's. Look at the state of this place." He tore a fresh piece of tape from the role and planted it across Mick's mouth before he had time to protest. "I'll be back in a minute, need to get the hoover."

Crates of milk and orange juice and bundles of unread newspapers bulging with magazine supplements lined the passageway leading to the downstairs utility room. Patrick had stripped to his love-heart boxer shorts and was rummaging through presses searching for washing powder. After successfully completing his mission and banging on a load he went to get the vacuum cleaner. The cardboard box filled with various Halloween masks distracted him from his duties and like a kid, he couldn't help himself from selecting one, a Batman eye mask, and sticking it on.

"It's not who I am underneath but what I do that defines me," Patrick quoted in his best Bruce Wayne voice. In all his excitement he didn't hear the side door closing after someone had entered the building.

"Din din din din, Batman. Din din din, Batman," sang Patrick in a sequence known only to him as he climbed the stairs, lugging the hoover, dressed in his love-heart boxers and still wearing his mask. He kicked open the living-room door with his toe and jumped through the gap. "I'm here to clean up Gotham City," he announced, still in character. "Kapow, bam," he continued while throwing a few shapes before realising that there were two pairs of eyes now firmly fixed on him.

Mick, bound and gagged in his chair, was rocking wildly back and forth trying to break free. The second set of eyes belonged to Sandra, Mick's ex. She reminded Patrick of one of those vampire vixen types from the B movies of the seventies. Painted black lips set within a powdery white face with her jet black hair severely pulled back in a ponytail. She stood with her arms folded under barely covered breasts in a black dress that looked as if it had been spray painted on.

"Who the hell are you?" Sandra finally managed to say.

Patrick set the vacuum cleaner down and put one hand on his hip while slowly shaking his head. He pointed a finger menacingly at his adversary and calmly said, "I'm Mick's partner and who the hell are you, an extra from the Addams' Family?"

Mick was almost having an apocalyptic fit. He bounced precariously from side to side in his chair, trying to be heard through his gag. Sandra gave a sorrowful scowl, appalled at what she was witnessing. She glared at her ex and said, "I knew there was something funny going on." She started to leave the room but suddenly stopped and turned her head. Mick shook in his chair like a man possessed.

"I'd have had far more respect if you were at least honest about your perversions," Mortitia said, "And to think that I wanted to get back with you."

Patrick put a hand to the side of his face, aghast.

"Have you been two-timin' me?" he asked Mick.

The shopkeeper was now chomping like a rabid dog on his gag, desperate to explain what was really happening and that he was in serious need of help.

"I'm taking the rest of my clothes but you can keep the dress. God knows what you've got up to in it," Sandra said, screwing up her face, having heard and seen enough.

Patrick followed Sandra down the stairs as she tried not to break her neck in her high heels. Watching her descend

129

reminded him of a packed mule negotiating its way down a steep ravine like in the cowboy films he loved so much as a child. She was burdened with several black plastic bags containing the contents of her wardrobe and almost toppled over in her haste to escape.

Patrick stuck his head out the side door and watched her fleeing. "And stay away from my man, ye home wrecker," he shouted after her.

The only sound filling the upstairs living-room was coming from a football match on the television and it was getting on Patrick's wick. It wasn't as torturous as a dripping tap but it was a very close second. He looked over at the sullen shopkeeper. Although the gag had been removed Mick was still confined by his restraints.

"Yer man's an awful waste of space altogether and the money they paid for him," Patrick said.

Mick ignored him.

"Ah yer not still in the horrors are ye?" asked Patrick.

The shopkeeper looked up at the ceiling.

"So yer not a transvestite after all," said Patrick, not trying to be mean but wanting Mick to engage in conversation. It worked.

The prisoner glared at him and said, "For the last damn time, no!"

Delighted with the breakthrough, Patrick decided to push on in his own uniquely subtle way.

"Well it wouldn't have bothered me in the slightest and people are far too quick to judge," he genuinely answered, "So wha' happened between yis then?"

Mick didn't answer but his reddening cheeks betrayed him.

"Don't tell me, someone else was givin' her a portion?" Patrick said.

"Something like that," Mick reluctantly answered, hoping against hope that his captor would just shut the hell up and let it go.

"Never mind, plenty of other mots out there. Wha' about yer wan that works for ye?"

"Tina?" said Mick, momentarily forgetting his own personal woes.

"She's a fine bit of stuff all the same."

"I was working on it before somebody ruined it for me," the shopkeeper said, raising an eyebrow.

"The dirty fecker," Patrick said, completely missing the accusation, "Not to worry, women are mad for the dosh and yer rollin' in it so ye'll be grand." He nodded towards a plastic bag on the table which he'd left lying there, earlier on. "Are ye not goin' to ask me what's in the bag?"

"No."

"Ah, go on?"

Mick threw his eyes to the heavens and said, "What's in the bag?"

"A surprise," Patrick said, trying to create a sense of excitement.

The other man looked blankly at him.

"Are ye not even a little bit curious?" asked Patrick, indicating something small with his thumb and index finger.

The shopkeeper's face remained uninterested. "Not particularly," he said.

Patrick got to his feet, making a fuss. "Ye can be so ungrateful at times and all I do be doin' for ye." He grabbed the bag and held it out. "I was only thinkin' about the long, lonely nights and the way ye live like a hermit."

"Excuse me," Mick interrupted. "I have plenty of company when I'm not being held prisoner by deranged lunatics such as yourself."

"Jaysus, pal, I think that's a bit harsh," Patrick said, "But under the circumstances I'm not gonna hold it against ye. Break-ups can be tough." He produced a game console from the bag and held it aloft. "Dah-dah."

Child-like laughter filled the upstairs living-room, a vast contrast to the terse atmosphere of late. Patrick was sat cross legged on the floor playing Mario Kart as the bemused shopkeeper looked on, barely hiding his contempt for the imbecile. The outstretched controller in Patrick's hands was turned one way then the other as he attempted to steer the onscreen car around various obstacles while his upper body subconsciously mirrored his hand movements. He checked over his shoulder and shouted, "This is a lot harder than it looks." When he glanced back at the screen his car had crashed. "Ah shite, I was just gettin' the bleedin' hang of it and all." He offered the controller to Mick. "Yer turn, bud."

His prisoner point blankly refused to take it, giving him a withering look instead.

"Suit yerself," said Patrick, "I'll have to take yer turn for ye."

No sooner had he said this when he let out a girlish shriek as Mick's racing character smashed into a barrier and died. Patrick turned to his prisoner and laughed, "Sure yer worse than me."

"Unbelievable," muttered Mick.

"If I'm bein' honest here, pal, I don't think ye were even tryin'," Patrick said, setting the controller on the floor. He clapped his hands loudly, sprung to his feet and said, "I think we'll give it a break until later, me poxy thumbs are killin' me."

Mick looked but didn't bother to engage with his captor. He was too busy milling things around inside his head trying to figure out a way to end this nightmare before he went completely looney tunes.

"How's about we do some serious retail therapy instead?" said Patrick, producing a credit card from his pocket like a well practised magician and holding it up for inspection. "Michael J. Flynn," he read aloud.

His disinterested prisoner was all of a sudden very keen.

"Where did you get that?" the shopkeeper asked, flabbergasted.

"Found it," Patrick nonchalantly answered, "Not that I was snoopin' around or anythin' sneaky like that," he said, wagging his finger, "I have boundaries ye know."

"Give it back, I'm warning you," Mick loudly said, clearly agitated by the whole scenario.

His captor dismissed him with a wave of his hand. "Don't be worryin', sure my share of the jackpot will more than cover any minor shoppin' expenses."

Mick wasn't having any of it. "Give it back," he shouted, his nostrils visibly flaring.

Patrick fetched the adhesive tape and plastered Mick's mouth having heard enough.

"Stop the frettin', everything's under control," he said.

Chapter 9

Friday.

"Heartburn's a fecker," Patrick declared after waking up with an awful tangy taste in his mouth accompanied by a burning sensation in his chest. The bottle of wine, a six-pack of cans and the ten packets of mixed flavoured crisps had been a great idea at the time. He gave his stomach a soothing rub, something his Ma used to do for him when he had a sickly or windy belly as a small boy. Conversation for the rest of the previous evening had been stifled to say the least. He couldn't understand Mick's protestations with regards to their credit card spending spree especially when they'd both be rolling in it soon enough. Trying to focus on the positives rather than Mick's negativities, he decided that a lovely fry-up would be a good start to the new day and would have the shopkeeper right as rain in no time at all. Patrick swung his legs over the side of the bed and tentatively tried to touch the floor with the tips of his toes. Satisfied that there was indeed terra firma despite the feeling of being at sea, he placed his feet firmly on the floor and rose ever so slowly. He concentrated and took a small step forward which under the circumstances was a giant leap for a man in his state. He managed to make his way downstairs and cautiously popped his head outside the front door breathing in the cool fresh air. He immediately recognised the man who was fast asleep in the doorway in a foetal position on a torn section of cardboard. It was his new friend, homeless Larry.

Patrick flicked through the dated Yellow Pages watched closely by Mick.

"Ye should think about gettin' yerself a gold card or somethin'," Patrick suggested, absentmindedly, "The limit on that other one maxed out in no time at all and I only bought a coupla plane tickets, some exercise equipment and a few other bits and pieces."

Mick was feeling well and truly deflated and decided to keep his mouth shut.

"Ah, here we are," Patrick said, holding his finger on an ad in the Pet Shops section.

A gentle knock was heard on the living-room door. Mick immediately twisted his neck in its direction, praying for salvation at last.

"Come in," said Patrick, raising his voice slightly. He didn't seem to be in the least bit surprised.

The door slowly opened and Larry appeared, freshly washed and shaven and looking about ten years younger. He was dressed in a bathrobe several sizes too big.

"Sit down me aul flower, I've done ye a bit of grub," Patrick warmly said, pointing towards the table where Mick was tied.

Larry shuffled across the room to take his seat but was slightly embarrassed to make eye contact with the grumpy owner.

"You'll catch flies if ye don't shut that," Patrick said, referring to Mick's gaping mouth.

"What the hell is he doing here?" the shopkeeper eventually managed to ask. "God knows what diseases he might be carrying."

Patrick shook his head disappointedly and said, "Is that any way to treat a neighbour?" He looked at his guest. "I have to apologise for that clown's outburst, Larry. Was the water hot enough for ye?"

"Anything's warmer than the Duck's pond," the older man answered.

Patrick smiled and said, "I'll have to take yer word for that."

'Can things possibly get any worse?' the shopkeeper thought.

The mobile phone was cradled between Patrick's ear and shoulder as he fiddled with the lonely few coins that were left in the till along with a substantial pile of I.O.U's. Lying open on the counter was the Yellow Pages that he'd been routing through earlier on and which he'd marked with a large dog ear on the pet shops section. Saying his mother wouldn't have been impressed would have been an understatement. She was a very kind and gentle woman but he could remember as if it was only yesterday when he'd put a dog ear on a library book. That was a cardinal sin. She'd given him both barrels before taking the iron to the page in an attempt to remove or at least lessen the crease. He still missed his Ma and the passage of time had only made it a small bit more bearable. A voice on the other end of the phone line jolted him back to the here and now.

"Three hundred and forty euro, that's dayligh' robbery," Patrick exclaimed, "We're only talkin' about a few sheets of glass here, bud."

The voice was not for turning.

"Yer aul wan wasn't Thatcher by any chance?" Patrick sarcastically asked.

Another grumbled response followed before Patrick decided to let it go and pay the price.

"Yeah, of course I want the tank, me fish needs space," he said.

He hung up and scratched his chin. He needed time to contemplate his next move. Larry, carrying a coffee, ambled into the shop from the backroom, dressed in his old clothes which looked a lot fresher having been washed and dried.

"Thanks for doin' me stuff," he said.

"Yer more than welcome. I'll get ye a few new bits and pieces later on once I raise a bit of cash," Patrick said.

Larry smiled and said, "There's no need. These aul things do me just fine, I've grown into them. Besides, if I was to wear anything new it'd probably only be torn off me back."

"Is it that bad out there?"the younger man asked.

"Can be. There's a lot of decent skins too."

Patrick was embarrassed that he'd never given much thought to those forced to live rough on the streets.

"I didn't think you'd go ahead with it, ye know," said Larry.

"What's that?" asked Patrick.

"Borrowing the lottery machine and playing it for free?"

The younger man gave a mischievous smile and said, "Ah ye know wha' I'm like. Once I get an idea there's no stoppin' me."

"Ye must be really desperate for money," Larry said.

Patrick shrugged his shoulders and replied, "Sure who isn't?"

Larry let out a rasping cough that seemed to rattle his entire frame.

"Are ye alrigh'?" Patrick asked, genuinely concerned for his guest. "Will I get ye a doctor or somethin'?"

The older man held the palm of his hand up in a stalling motion until the coughing had subsided. He then wiped the tears from the corners of his eyes before speaking again. "Yer grand, son, a small bit of bronchitis, it'll soon settle."

"Are ye sure yer ok?"

"I'm absolutely positive," said Larry. He looked Patrick square in the eyes, trying to work him out. "I was once like you, ye know. Thought money was the B all and end all of everythin'. That was until I had it, then I found out that what I really craved was somethin' entirely different."

"I'm not followin' ye," Patrick said, giving a barely discernable shake of the head.

"I wasted so much time worryin' about money that when I finally had enough I'd lost what really mattered to me."

Patrick gave him a quizzical look.

"My family," explained Larry. "I became a stranger in my own home. To be honest, in the end I couldn't stand being in the same room as the kids, spoilt, selfish so-and-sos. And as for the wife, she found love in another man's arms."

"Sorry to hear that," said Patrick, commiserating with the man.

"Not that I blamed her," Larry added.

Patrick pulled a face.

"I suppose he was bleedin' loaded?"

Larry gave a wry chuckle. "That's the irony of it all. He was just an ordinary Joe Soap who stacked shelves for a living in the local supermarket. Didn't even have his own car."

"That's bananas."

"They were my exact thoughts too. I remember as clear as day asking the wife what was so special about yer man? What had he got that I didn't? And do you what she said?"

Patrick shook his head, completely baffled.

"Time for her. She said she married me for me and that while all the extra trappings were nice they were no replacement for loneliness."

"Jaysus," the younger man said. He let Larry's words sink in before opening his gob again. "So wha' did ye do?"

"The only decent thing I could. I walked away," admitted Larry. He subconsciously massaged his aching chest with his free hand before adding, "One small bit of advice. Money might seem like the answer to all yer troubles but if yer not careful it can cause an awful lot more." He set his empty coffee cup gently down on the counter. "I've gotta go."

"Ye don't have to..."

"I know," Larry said, "And thanks again for showing me that someone still cares in this world."

Patrick shuffled awkwardly.

"Remember, money's not everything," the older man added and was gone out the door, content that he'd made the right decision all those years ago.

Chapter 10

Patrick was faced with a massive dilemma. He still had a lot of things that he wanted to buy but the cash in the till had all but dried up. Although he'd no experience in the retail sector other than filling cars with fuel or washing them clean, he'd decided to open up the shop for an hour or two to earn some real money. After putting on one of the Halloween masks he'd found earlier, a gruesome kind of half rotten pumpkin, he was ready to face the world. He cautiously parted the venetian blinds and peeked out onto the street, checking left then right. All was quiet. He removed the 'Apologies for closure' notice which he'd seemed to have written such a long time ago and turned the closed sign to open.

Apart from the odd queer look and a bit of slagging about his disguise, the retail experience was going well enough. That was put to a serious test however when two local battleaxes with almost fluorescent blue rinses rambled in, dragging their two wheeled trolleys after them.

"And the puss that came out," said Bernie, the broader of the two.

"I can only imagine," replied Mary, her spectacle wearing counterpart, her faced screwed up in disgusted delight.

Bernie wasn't finished telling her story. "Her husband nearly fain..."

"Hello, ladies," said Patrick, albeit a bit louder than he meant to.

Bernie and Mary ceased their conversation mid sentence and looked at him with all the suspicion reserved for an axe murderer. Not one to beat around the bush, Bernie went straight for the jugular.

"Who are you when you're at home?" she asked.

"Eh, Mick the owner's brother," Patrick replied. He couldn't believe that he hadn't already prepared himself for such a basic question.

"What's your name then?" said Mary, sensing blood.

"John, John Boy. The good lookin' one," answered Patrick with a small laugh, hoping to throw them off the scent.

Neither Bernie nor Mary looked convinced.

"Hmm," said Mary, scratching the mole on her fuzzy chin. "What's with the mask?"

"Halloween?" said Patrick. "Happens on the thirty first of October every year?"

He gave a little chuckle but he wasn't winning any fans.

"You're a bit premature?" said Mary.

'Story of my life,' thought Patrick.

"A pagan festival," tutted Bernie, "Can't understand how it was ever allowed to grow into such an unsavoury and grotesque spectacle."

The stand-in shopkeeper chastised himself for his smartness knowing that he'd have to play it very carefully from here on in with Agatha Christy and her sidekick invention, Miss Marple. Bernie turned her head round and surveyed the place, setting her sights on a bunch of bananas which were more black than yellow.

"I see the standard of cleanliness is falling," she remarked.

"Next to Godliness, you know?" Mary said, sticking her oar in.

"My sincerest apologies, ladies," Patrick said, shaking his head while feigning disappointment. He marched over to the rotting bananas and promptly dumped them in a bin behind the counter. "I'm havin' awful trouble with the staff," he apologised.

"Am not surprised hiring Jezebels but it's still no excuse," Bernie said, narrowing her beady eyes at Patrick. She was obviously not a big fan of Tina's.

"I mean it's not as if the prices are any cheaper than up the road," Mary added.

Bernie left out an exaggerated sigh. "Probably dearer if the truth be told," she said, "Sure we only shop here to support the smaller man." She gave Patrick a withering look.

He smiled broadly behind the mask. This was a formidable duo but he was thoroughly enjoying the challenge.

"Funny ye should mention prices," he said, as a radical thought popped into his head.

Bernie and Mary instinctively leaned forward as one, sensing an offer.

"Because it just so happens that we're doin' a special today," he revealed.

The once heavily wrinkled faces of the older ladies

seemed to vanish in an instance, replaced instead by younger, more eager visages.

"A special?" they both responded, barely able to contain themselves.

Patrick slowly lifted his arms and raised the palms of his hands to the heavens, in a solemn, evangelistic kind of way.

"Yes indeed," he confirmed before handing each of the mesmerised ladies an empty basket. "Ye get one minute, a whole sixty seconds, to put whatever ye can manage into yer basket and all for the measly sum of ten euro each."

Bernie pulled back a fraction, her expression suddenly becoming more cautious. She'd been around a long time and wasn't easily fooled.

"What's the catch?" she asked.

Patrick gave a hearty laugh and said, "How fast can ye run?"

Bernie and Mary had thrown off their coats and rolled up their sleeves before picking up their shopping baskets and tearing around the place with surprising agility and speed. The rosy cheeked women grabbed random items from the shelves in a panic as the clock ticked down.

Patrick checked his watch and shouted, "Ten, nine, eight, seven..."

Less than twenty minutes after Bernie and Mary had first entered Flynn's Mini-Mart they emerged with their two wheeled trolleys in tow, laden down with their newly acquired goods and all for the paltry sum of ten euro. Although breathless, they looked years younger.

"A lovely chap all the same," Bernie said, complementing Patrick, "Charismatic."

"Could teach that sourpuss brother of his a thing or two," Mary added in praise.

"Reminded me in a way of Cary Grant, ye know," Bernie said, even though Patrick hadn't removed his pumpkin mask disguise. She was feeling a bit giddy for the first time in who knew how long. 'Her Frankie was going to be in for a bit of a surprise when she got hold of him later on,' she thought.

Mick sat alone in the upstairs flat, tied to his chair, listening intently to the boisterous laughter and shouting coming from below. It sounded as if there were at least a hundred people in his shop such was the volume and the associated commotion. His eyes flickered madly as he tried to guess what was going on and hoping that the Guards would be called to investigate. He would surely then be rescued, wouldn't he? He'd almost lost count of how many days he'd now been imprisoned but still hoped and prayed, not that he was in any way religious. As the saying went, 'there were no atheists in a foxhole.' He'd even started to convince himself that he had a kind of kinship with that Nelson Mandela guy. Of course Mandela had been banged away on Robben Island for a bit longer, almost two decades in fact but their similar circumstances could not be underestimated.

A large and rather rowdy mob had gathered outside the front of the mini-mart, bustling with one another to try and see how the next 'contestant' was getting on. Word had spread like wildfire in the area about the mad fella in the local shop running a version of the supermarket sweep. Hidden behind his pumpkin head mask, Patrick stood guard at the entrance with his back to the crowd, holding a crisp ten euro note in his hand. He watched with glee as an athletic young man raced up and down the aisles swinging an overflowing shopping basket. As he tore past the toiletries section his footing went from under him and try as he might he couldn't avoid crashing into the rack stacked with fine wines from all over the world. Upstairs, Mick strained forward listening to the sound of bottles smashing. The mob was stunned into silence until the young man emerged from the pile of broken glass with a beaming smile, holding aloft a perfectly intact bottle of Faustino V Rioja. The roar that followed was like a goal being scored in an All-Ireland final.

The day's takings were far better than Patrick had anticipated and it had afforded him the opportunity to purchase a few extra pieces for Jaws' new abode. As he studied the instructions which had come with the fish tank he could feel Mick burning a hole into the side of his head. Patrick turned round and looked questioningly at the grump tied to the chair.

"Have ye a problem?" he asked, trying not to let the moany hole get him down.

"Yes I fucking do. What do you mean you opened my shop?" Mick said, his jaw tensed to the last.

"Less of the profanities there, like a good man," Patrick calmly replied. "I even ran a little promotion and it was very successful," he said, seeing no wrong in what he had done. "You should think of doin' somethin' similar when you're back at work and I don't mind givin' ye a few tips."

The shopkeeper was furious. "I heard glass breaking," he said.

Patrick slapped the fish tank brochure against his thigh and said, "I think yer blowin' things outta all proportion, bud."

"You think so?"

Patrick waved his arm dismissively but in a friendly sort of way and said, "Yeah, nothin' to worry about. A few minutes with a hoover and the shop'll be brand new."

"I don't want you opening up again."

"I can't make any promises," Patrick replied with a smile. "But with a small bit of luck I won't have to. I know it's tough and that yer used to bein' in charge but ye just have to trust me."

The shopkeeper let out a frustrated sigh. "You haven't got a clue," he said.

"Wha' are ye on about now?" asked Patrick.

"What tough really means," said Mick.

The atmosphere in the room changed in an instant. Patrick didn't like where this conversation was going and decided to put his prisoner back in his box.

"Oh I know exactly wha' it means," he said, biting down on his lip. "I seen me poor Ma after me Da died, strugglin' to keep her head above water, workin' for shit arses like you." He pointed his finger at the shopkeeper so he was under no illusion as to who he was speaking to.

"That's not fair," said Mick, "You don't even know me."

Patrick wasn't finished just yet. "Yer Daddy probably gave ye the shop for yer birthday."

"How dare you," shouted the prisoner, "I was orphaned at ten and adopted by an uncle who only ever saw me as free labour."

"Stop the roarin', will ye," Patrick said, taken aback by the shopkeeper's revelation. "Look, I'm sorry, all righ'."

Tears began to well up in Mick's eyes.

"Ah don't start all that bleedin' malarkey again," said Patrick, "All ye've done since I've gotten here is complain and to be honest with ye, I've had it up to here." He put his hand to his forehead to show just how much he had it up to.

"I don't believe I'm hearing this," Mick said, shaking his head.

Patrick let out an exaggerated breath and said, "There ye go again. And after all I've done for ye."

Mick gave a derisive snort.

"Anyone else would have left ye sittin' in yer dirty jocks," Patrick continued.

"If you hadn't tied me up to begin with…" said Mick.

"And as for the meals I went to the trouble of makin' for ye. Well, fatso, ye can starve for the rest of the week for all I care. I'm gettin' outta here."

Mick suddenly leaned forward, extremely concerned at the sudden turn of events.

"Where are you going?" he asked.

"Somewhere I don't have to listen to you constantly gabbin' on..."

"But what about me?" the shopkeeper asked in a panic.

Patrick slowly shook his head. "See. Me, me, me. Maybe I won't come back and ye can sit there and rot."

"Stop, don't go. I'll be quiet, you won't even know I'm here," Mick pleaded.

Patrick ignored his prisoner and made for the door.

"Please?" the shopkeeper repeated.

Patrick paused and turned. "Okay, I'll come back," he said.

Panic flickered across the other man's eyes. "You're not still going are you?" he asked.

"Ye better believe it, pal. This is way too stressful for me," Patrick replied, already leaving the room.

"Don't go," Mick said in disbelief.

The door closed behind his captor.

"Don't go," he shouted.

The door opened again and Mick let out a sigh of relief. Patrick strode past his hostage, tore a strip from the roll of adhesive tape and plastered it across his prisoner's gaping mouth. He then left, almost skipping out the door. The shopkeeper listened intently, hoping against hope that this was just an idle threat and that his captor was only winding him up just to make a point. Unfortunately for Mick he soon realised that Patrick was serious when he heard the side door slam shut. Paralysed with fear his mind went blank.

A giant cocktail glass lit up with powerful red and blue LED lighting caught Patrick's eye as he shuffled down the busy cobbled street, dodging exuberant revellers. He paused outside the swanky bar and decided to go in even though he didn't usually frequent places like this. He definitely preferred the comfort and safety of the 'old man' pubs not to mention that they almost always served a better class of pint. This was the sort of place Mandy, his ex, would rave about. She loved the gin glasses which were big enough to double up as fish bowls. The trouble with Mandy was that she drank like a fish too and on his meagre salary that was always going to be a struggle. It wasn't that he didn't like spending money. No, the opposite was in fact true. He loved to throw cash around, the problem was he hadn't got any most of the time. A group of young women were having their I.D's checked by the burly doorman when Patrick decided to brush past as if he was a regular and hadn't got time for this sort of nonsense. The vibe he gave off seemed to work as the bouncer stepped aside and let him pass with a gruff nod. Forcing his way to the bar through the packed and giddy crowd, Patrick couldn't help trampling on a few toes along the way and having to smile apologetically over the loud music while pointing towards the beer taps. Most people understood and gave a sympathetic nod knowing only too well what an epic struggle it could be trying to get served but he still got a few snooty looks. After finally managing to get the barman's attention he made sure to pick up two bottles to delay repeating the process. He'd chosen some fancy named stuff from Latin America with a bit of lime shoved down the neck not trusting the stout on draught. He took a swig from one of the bottles and it tasted surprisingly good. Surveying the packed bar, he was envious of the loved up couples and the carefree attitudes of the patrons in general. Out of the corner of his eye he spotted an absolute stunner sitting further along the counter. Some tanned guy in a snug fitting shirt that actually fit perfectly over his toned physique was chatting her up. Although she laughed Patrick could tell that she was having none of it. The chap in the nice shirt eventually got the hint and slipped away to lick his wounds, hoping to find a capture elsewhere before the night was out. Taking this as his cue, Patrick sidled up to the gorgeous lady while trying to look indifferent. He took another swig of his drink and had no sooner removed his mouth when the beer bubbled up and erupted over the top and onto the floor. His potential target gave him a look that had 'pathetic' written all over it. Undeterred, Patrick edged closer.

"I see Rodger Ramjet got shot down in flames," he said, nodding towards the good looking chap in the nice shirt who had already locked onto another potential target.

"Hmm. Don't take this the wrong way," the woman said, "But does your Mammy know you're out this late?"

"Sorry?" replied Patrick.

"No need to be," said the stunner, "Now run along home like a good boy before you get into any more trouble." She turned her back on the nuisance and exhaled loudly not bothering to hide her contempt.

Patrick was stunned at first at the woman's directness but slowly regained his composure. He took a risk and tapped her on the shoulder. She slowly turned her head round and glared at him.

"I'll have ye know that my mother's dead and that I have me own shop," he said. The words had escaped his big mouth before he could stop them.

The stunner narrowed her eyes as the tip of her tongue slowly worked its way along her lower lip. "You?" she hissed.

Now that he had started this line of spoofing he felt he had no other option but to continue.

"Yeah," he boastfully said, "It's a newsagent's and mini-market all under the one roof and it does a flyin' trade."

'A man of means, this could be interesting,' the woman thought. She twisted round fully on her smooth, red leather circular seat, flashing a generous amount of tanned leg.

"And who's the lucky woman then?" she asked, probing for more info.

"Wha' do ye mean?" asked Patrick, not quite up to speed.

"Your wife, what's her name?"

"I don't have one," Patrick answered defensively.

The stunner sized him up and said, "So you're single then."

"That's very presumptuous," said Patrick, trying to be smart and modern, "I could have a fella."

"Honey, trust me, no one would ever mistake you for being gay," she said, rolling her eyes to heaven, "Just look at the state of you. I mean, I've seen better fashion on down and outs who rely on skips to dress them."

Patrick took a swig of his drink and was about to move off when the woman held out her hand.

"The name's Tina by the way," she said, fluttering her extended eyelashes, "So what's yours, handsome?"

The conversation flowed surprisingly well between Patrick and Tina thanks in no small part to the copious amounts of drink being drank, mostly on Tina's behalf. She subconsciously flicked her gleaming hair to one side every now and then, resembling something out of one of those glamorous shampoo ads. Patrick couldn't help but notice the admiring looks he was getting from blokes passing and could almost hear them think 'lucky bastard.' He also got the eye from a couple of cute ladies, something which never happened in the past. He supposed it was a bit like that saying the career guidance teacher in his old school was always hammering on about, 'It's far easier to get a job when you already have one!'

Back at the flat, things weren't going quite as smoothly for Mick. Whatever way he'd moved earlier his back had gone into spasms and the pain was excruciating. The rumbling from his stomach also reminded him that he hadn't eaten in hours and he was absolutely ravenous. To make matters worse there was a scrumptious looking slice of cake sitting tantalisingly close by on the kitchen table, waving at him. Like a petulant child not getting their own way, he began to rock back and forth furiously, a layer of sweat forming on his brow. He somehow managed to tumble forward and twist in the air before landing sideways on the ground. He was momentarily winded and lay still until he could properly catch his breath. Knowing that this was probably going to be his best and only chance to get free, he immediately started to work on his taped mouth not quite sure how long he'd have. His jaws moved this way and that, like some crazed drug addict mad out of his head on gear. He was going to earn his freedom and get revenge but not before having his cake and eating it too.

"D'ye wanna salt and vinegar on yer chips?" the stocky lad with the greased back hair asked from behind the hot fryers.

Patrick shrugged his shoulders. "D'ye want salt and vinegar?" he said, turning round to where he'd left Tina resting on the tiled ledge with her back against the large, reinforced glass window.

"Yeah, whatever," she replied as she slid along the glass about to fall over.

Patrick raced over and managed to catch her just before she hit the floor and did some real damage. He sat her upright again, held a hand either side of her shoulders to steady her before tentatively retreating a few steps.

"What is he like?" Tina said to the other merry customers who were also waiting for grub.

"Ahh, he must be madly in love with ye," replied an elderly man with an amorous smile. He then attempted to put an arm around his wife who was standing next to him in the queue but received a discreet dig in the ribs for his troubles.

"Ow, wha' was that for?" he asked indignantly.

His wife put on a fake smile as if it was all fun and games but everyone knew she was going to throttle him once she got him home. Happy that Tina wasn't going anywhere for the next few seconds at least, Patrick went back to the counter. He noticed the chipper man pursing his lips admiringly, taking in Tina's beauty even though she was three sheets to the wind.

"Battered sausage," the chipper man said.

"No, just the three bags of chips, please," said Patrick.

The chipper man laughed and said, "No, that's what I would have if she was mine."

Patrick gave a quick glance over his shoulder at Tina who was once again beginning to slide along the glass. He turned back to the chipper man. "Well she's not," he said, grabbing the chips off the counter. He helped his date to her feet and linked her arm, needing all of his strength to escort her out of the shop.

The chipper guy shook his head, envious of the fun and frolics going to be had by the couple or at least the lucky bloke.

There were plenty of taxis whizzing past as Patrick tried to hail a ride but they were either full or racing to call-outs. He deposited Tina against a railing with her bag of chips, most of which were completely missing her mouth and ending up on the path. An abandoned mongrel dog which looked absolutely starved was delighted with the windfall. Another few cabs passed by before an eight-seater Japanese import finally pulled in.

"C'mon, are ye righ'?" Patrick called to Tina, not wanting the driver to change his mind.

"Give me a hand," slurred Tina, struggling to get to her feet.

He knew she'd had more than a few but he didn't think she was that bad. One minute she was all chat and cosying up to him, quizzing him on how much 'his' shop turned over in an average week, the next thing he knew she could barely string a sentence together or stop herself from slipping off of her stool.

Moments after bundling Tina into the rear of the taxi she left out an enormous belch that would have brought tears of joy to any Arab chef worth their salt.

The driver whipped his head round and glared at the smiling couple.

"She better not get sick and don't be eatin' them chips in me car," he warned.

"No problem, bud," Patrick said, trying to reassure the driver, "The rest of them are for me pal in anyway."

"That was gas," giggled Tina in a voice she mistakenly took for being hushed. She rested her head on Patrick's shoulder. "A shopkeeper, I knew it was going to be my lucky night."

Patrick hated that he'd lied about owning a shop but it proved his point once again about being a nobody unless you had money. He glanced sideways at the stunner who now had her eyes closed and was gently purring in peace.

It was an entirely different story back at Flynn's mini-mart. The door leading from the back room into the shop was slowly pushed open to reveal a place in total disarray. Various items, including broken wine bottles and fruit were scattered across the tiled floor while the majority of the shelves, sitting at skewered angles, were bereft of stock. Mick took a step forward crushing glass beneath his shoe. He surveyed the chaos and was absolutely enraged. All of his years of hard work had been thrashed in a matter of days. He bent down and picked up a lemon, holding it aloft in his hand. This was the final straw. He squashed the piece of fruit, crushing it to a pulp as if it was a mere grape.

Patrick had Tina draped over his shoulder in a fireman's lift. He was doing his best to balance her and the chips whilst also trying to slide the key into the side door lock. He felt like that Luke Skywalker geezer when he was trying to lock-on to the tiny target on the evil Death Star. Tina made a sudden move causing him to almost drop his date on her head but managed to somehow pin her against the door just in time. 'It could have been worse,' he jokingly thought to himself, 'he'd nearly let the chips fall too.'

He just about managed to get Tina safely inside the building while also doing his best to keep the noise to a minimum. For some unknown reason the hairs on the back of his neck suddenly stood on end. He listened intently for almost a minute but could hear nothing apart from Tina's gentle murmurings. It had been a long day he told himself and he was just imagining things. The stairs appeared to be a lot steeper than before as he hauled his inebriated date up to the bedroom. Breathless, he toe-poked the door and with a last burst of strength managed to toss Tina onto the bed. She stirred a little and her glazed eyes opened.

"You're keen," she said but almost immediately the lids slid down and she was out for the count once again. Patrick took a step back and admired the gorgeous woman stretched out on the bed. She was built for sin alright, there was no doubting that. Her vulnerability also added to her beauty. He lustfully imagined going a few rounds with this one but then immediately felt ashamed for having such thoughts when she was clearly drunk and not in control of her actions. Maybe when she sobered up they might be able to pick up from where they'd left off, several gallons of gin earlier. He gently removed her Christian Louboutin stilettos with the red underside which she'd earlier informed him on more than one occasion had cost her an absolute fortune. It sounded very impressive when he'd promised to buy her a couple more pairs. She'd told him she was going to hold him to it. He left her shoes at the foot of the bed then tenderly covered her stunning figure with the duvet and backing away. He collected the chips on his way out.

"All righ', bud. Got ye somethin' from the chipper," Patrick said, heading into the living-room where he'd left Mick hours earlier to stew, "As a peace offerin' like."

The empty chair was lying sideways on the floor with the rope restraints and adhesive tape abandoned next to it. He slowly set the takeaway food down on the table and edged towards the toppled chair. He noticed what looked like blood stains on some of the ropes and bent down on his hunkers to inspect things further. A sudden noise somewhere in the building put his heart sideways. He jumped up and quickly scanned the room, looking for something, anything, to arm himself with. A poker hanging from a brass holder next to a decorative pan and brush caught his eye. He rubbed his chin not really sure if this was the right way to go about things but then convinced himself that it was way easier to negotiate if you were tooled up. With the metal rod now firmly gripped in his right hand he cautiously popped his head out of the room, checking one way then the other.

After being cooped up for so long it took Mick's body a while to adjust to his new found freedom. His muscles ached from doing nothing and he was brought to tears as his calf cramped in a spasm as he'd descended the stairs almost causing him to take a tumble. Now that he was fully mobile again he set his sights on getting revenge. He popped the lid open on his toolbox knowing exactly what he was looking for. A claw hammer had many uses but he was positive you'd never find it advertised anywhere describing what he intended to do with it.

Patrick crept down the stairs after doing a sweep of the top floor. All was going well until he stood on a step which left out a groaning creak similar to that of a sinking ship. He immediately lifted his foot and froze, cursing his clumsiness under his breath while hoping to Jaysus that he hadn't been heard. Nothing stirred for what felt like an age. Cautiously, he continued his descent. He came to the door that led into the shop and took a deep breath. He used the tip of poker to push it open. Preparing to be ambushed he quickly retreated and raised his weapon in readiness. Nothing untoward happened. Feeling a bit braver he leaned forward and scanned the shop. Although it resembled the aftermath of some wild music festival after his supermarket sweep promotion, nothing else seemed to be out of place. He'd seen enough scary movies in his time to know that he was probably better off turning on his heels and getting the hell out of dodge but for some reason he entered the room. Although he knew it was ridiculous the aisles appeared much longer to him as he edged forward, half crouching. He came to the end of the row and sneaked a look round the corner. His eyes were drawn towards the brand new, illuminated fish tank sitting on the counter which had cost a small fortune. A glint of light mid tank somehow looked out of place. He was inexplicably drawn towards it, not able to fully process what was wrong with the picture he was seeing. His beloved fish, Jaws, was speared by a sharp knife, the point of which was embedded in the treasure chest resting on the bottom. A faint trace of blood seeping from the wound was causing the water to grow cloudier. He crouched down and leaned his face towards the glass not quite believing the violence which had been inflicted upon this innocent animal.

"Jaws," he barely heard himself say. He placed a finger on the side of the tank, stroking it gently. Suddenly, another set of eyes appeared at the far side staring back at him. It was the shopkeeper. Both men slowly straightened up until they were now face to face above the tank. The shopkeeper wore a demonic look. The blood stains around his mouth didn't help things either.

"Why?" asked Patrick, almost in tears, "Have ye no sense of fair play?"

Mick swung the claw hammer and it was lights out for Patrick.

Blinking rapidly, Patrick attempted to focus on his surroundings but the blurred pictures were spinning wildly. His head was thumping and he felt nauseous. He decided to shut his eyes tightly for a few moments before trying again. This time when he opened them the spinning had slowed to a gradual halt and the blurred images began to focus properly. The roles were now well and truly reversed. Mick, still wearing the red dress, sauntered into the room carrying a DVD in one hand and Jaws, still speared on the knife, in the other. He set the disc down on the table. Patrick glanced round and realised that he was tied to the wooden chair in the upstairs flat where he had held Mick captive the last few days. A nasty, perfectly circular, raised lump sat in the middle of his forehead looking like a small volcano that was liable to erupt at any moment.

"Thought you could do with the company," Mick said, grinning. He then forcefully stabbed the knife into the table.

Jaws momentarily swayed back and forth until the metal blade steadied itself. Patrick was absolutely appalled by the shopkeeper's barbaric behaviour especially after the way he had treated him so kindly since his arrival.

"Why haven't ye called the guards?" he shouted then immediately regretted it as he winced with the pain in his head.

Mick ignored his victim and produced a handgun instead.

"This look familiar?" he asked.

Patrick recognised the weapon as the one he had earlier threatened the shopkeeper with. He didn't flinch when it was pointed at him, knowing too well that it was only a fake gun which he'd picked up in a small ex-army clothing type store. Mick squeezed the trigger, blasting the prisoner into the face and eyes with the clear liquid.

"Ahh..." screamed Patrick, his eyes stinging with pain.

"Very convincing water pistol all the same," said Mick, "And completely harmless unless of course one decides to fill it with lemon juice that is." He casually strolled over to the table and set down the gun.

"Me eyes, ye bleedin' sap," Patrick roared, much to the shopkeeper's amusement. He blinked them rapidly hoping that his tears would dilute the citric acid. "Ye've completely lost the plot, I could be left blind or with ritna, retnul, eyeball damage or whatever it's bleedin' called."

Mick waved his hand dismissively and said, "It's nothing compared to the pain you've caused me these last few days."

Patrick's eyes were beginning to calm although he could still feel a burning sensation.

"At least I had a plan," he snarled.

Mick put a finger to his mouth. "Shush," he said, "I have one too." He picked up the disc from the table, stuck it into a machine and pressed play. The DVD contained footage from the discreet security camera fixed to the ceiling in a corner of the shop. The quality was excellent not like some of the ridiculous shite that you'd see on the crime prevention shows on television where even the perpetrator's own mother wouldn't recognise them. Patrick was curious as to what was going on but decided to keep quiet for the moment. On screen he could see himself entering the shop with Mick leaning into the chest fridge counting the ice creams. He was then shown moving towards Mick armed with the can of beans. 'All good so far,' thought Patrick, knowing what happened next although he was embarrassed that he'd even contemplated hurting someone in such a callous way. The footage next showed him raising the can about to wallop the unsuspecting shopkeeper. For some reason it suddenly jumped forward to where the shopkeeper was lying prone on the floor with Patrick standing over him with the tin of beans in his hand. There was no sound but he could clearly make out what he'd said, 'It's not wha' we do, it's the way that we do it!'

"That's not wha' really happened..." Patrick said, still a bit slow on the uptake.

Mick smiled and said, "It is now. You see, I'm going to carry on with your little lottery experiment just for the fun of it. And when it's all over I'll ring the Guards and let you try to explain things." He ejected the disc from the machine and placed it on the table. "Unless of course," he added, chuckling like some screwball, "I actually win the jackpot, in which case I'll have a few extra refuse sacks for the bin men."

Patrick was now decidedly worried at this latest turn of events.

Chapter 11

Saturday.

Time has an incredible way of playing tricks on the mind. Just like how tortuously slow it seems to drag when you're watching your favourite team hanging on to a one goal lead in the dying moments of a game or how quickly it seems to fly when you're away on holidays and having a ball. Somehow Mick and Patrick had both made it to Saturday, alive. The lotto machine was dutifully spitting out tickets as the shopkeeper, still wearing the dress, went about the business of cleaning up his shop. He dumped bunches of rotten bananas into an almost full refuse sack before knotting it tightly. Aside from the dreadful food waste Mick was still seething at the damage which the idiot tied to the chair in the room above had allowed to happen. He was definitely going to make him pay for it. A knock on the locked front door caught his attention. He'd left the sign in the window saying that they were closed due to a family illness so this was unexpected. Cautiously, he made his way over to the blinds and had a peek. He immediately recognised the scumbag dressed in the black baggy tracksuit pants and matching hooded top as an 'employee' of local gangster, Frank Harris. He decided to ignore the lowlife in the hope that he would just clear off but he knew in his heart that that was never going to happen. The scumbag banged on the glass door even louder this time. Mick reluctantly opened a large gap in the blinds.

"We're closed," he said without any real conviction.

Frank's man smiled.

165

"Open the fuckin' door before I put it in on top on ye," he threatened.

The shopkeeper gave it brief consideration before allowing the toe-rag to enter and locking the door again.

"Billy, isn't it?" he said, more out of habit than any great interest.

Billy looked him up and down.

"Nice dress," he said.

"Oh, this little thing," Mick nonchalantly replied, walking around to the far side of the counter, "I felt like letting a bit of air get at my nether regions, you know yourself."

Billy screwed up his face.

"Should be all put down, shams like you but that's just my honest opinion," he said.

Mick smiled and kept his cool. "Now there's a surprise."

"Anyways, I'm here for the bread," said Billy.

"The bread?" Mick asked, gripping the hammer which he had hidden next to the till.

Billy shuffled uncomfortably. There was something very different about the shop owner today. He was usually shitting a brick but his eyes were all over the shop as if he was on gear and he was acting very brave.

"Ye know, for Frank?" the thug said.

"Frank?" Mick said absentmindedly.

"Frank Harris?" repeated Billy, a lot less sure of himself than when he'd first entered the premises. "He told me to collect the bread?"

"Ah, okay," Mick replied, letting go of the hammer.

He walked round from the till and went down one of the aisles closely watched by Billy, picked up a slice pan before returning and setting it on the counter.

"It's not the freshest but should be okay if it's toasted. I've been a bit preoccupied these last few days. Would you like me to put it into a bag for you?" he asked.

"Wha'?"

"A plastic bag? Would you like me to put the bread into a plastic bag?" Mick repeated.

Billy looked unsure as to what the fuck was actually going on here.

"It will cost you an extra few cent," the shopkeeper said, "For the government's environmental tax. It's a nuisance I know but if it cuts down on litter..."

Billy slammed his fist down on the counter.

"Are ye takin' the piss?" he shouted.

Mick didn't flinch. "And you've got to admit, the bags look terrible stuck up in trees," he said, putting the slice pan into a plastic bag.

The scumbag had enough. He snatched the bread from the shopkeeper, roughly shaking the packaging and sending the slices flying everywhere.

"Put the fuckin' money in the bag ye queer bastard or I'll blow yer ugly mug off," he roared, regaining some of his earlier confidence. He pulled a gun from his waistband and pointed it at Mick.

The shopkeeper exhaled loudly but still remained calm.

"See that's what's wrong with your generation. Absolutely no imagination," he said.

Billy put the gun to Mick's head and cocked the trigger.

"Shut it, I'm fuckin' serious," he warned.

"Nor the slightest bit of originality, just like your awful taste in music," Mick continued unabated. "Boom, boom, boom, boom. Would give an Asperin a headache."

"I'm not gonna warn ye again," shouted Billy.

Mick picked up Patrick's imitation gun from under the counter and set it down on top in plain sight. Billy stared at the weapon and instantly recognised it as being an identical fake to his own. The shopkeeper secretly slid his hand around the handle of the hammer, gripping it tightly.

"If we were playing cards," he said, "This is where I'd say snap."

It was just as well that no one was passing the shop at that precise moment such was the scream which Billy left out as the hammer was brought violently down upon his forehead.

A feeling of empowerment washed over Mick after his earlier encounter with the scumbag. He swore that he would never again pay another cent in protection money to Frank Harris or any other parasite for that matter. The bottle of red wine he'd already downed had no doubt bolstered this new found courage. He lounged in the armchair with his dress now pulled off his shoulders and bunched up around his waist for comfort. Swigging directly from a second bottle of wine, he watched the Lotto presenter live on the television going through his routine. Patrick couldn't help but notice the massive pile of quick pick slips on the table. The shopkeeper noticed his prisoner's interest.

"I did a few extra, being a rollover and all of that jazz," Mick said, "And the powers that be half expect it."

"So I see," Patrick replied, trying his best to restrict his movements so his rope restraints wouldn't cut into him any further and completely cut off his circulation.

Onscreen, the camera closed in on the numbered balls obediently waiting in line to be rolled into action.

"This is it, show-time," Mick said, winking at his prisoner.

Patrick half smiled in return. The lotto balls were dropped into the clear drum and were sent milling about into a wild frenzy. The jackpot amount behind the presenter read seven million, six hundred and fifty-two thousand, nine hundred euro.

"Fifteen, nineteen, twenty-six, two, twenty-five, thirteen and the bonus number is four," the presenter announced as each ball was picked. He then wished the viewers the very best of luck and to always gamble responsibly. The irony wasn't lost on the shopkeeper.

"Did you hear that?" he taunted Patrick, "Gamble responsibly." He laughed meanly but his prisoner didn't take the bait.

Mick rose to his feet, switching the television over to the twitter.

"Care for a drink?" he asked.

Patrick shook his head 'no' and said, "Ye look very pleased with yerself?"

"Ten out of ten for the observation. Not bad for a guy with a shit load of 'isms'," Mick replied, grinning from ear to ear. "I did something today that I should have done a long time ago."

Although Patrick didn't want to engage any further with the arsehole the curiosity got the better of him.

"Wha' was that then?" he asked.

The shopkeeper threw a few punches as if he was shadow boxing then pretended to deliver a knockout blow. "I just hope that I'm still here when Mr. big boss man himself, Frank fucking Harris comes a calling. He'll be the one who needs protecting."

Despite the area around the upended wine rack being littered with pieces of coloured glass, Mick had somehow managed to find another bottle which was still intact. He stumbled into the upstairs living-room with his drink while also holding a large, unlit cigar in his mouth. He glanced over at the television to see if any winners had been announced but nothing was showing as of yet. He set the wine on the table and disappeared again without a word only to return moments later carrying a wooden ruler and pen. He tossed the stationary onto the table, retrieved his drink and flopped into his armchair.

"Right, we're all set then," he said.

The digital clock in the bottom right of the t.v. screen read 20.45.

Tina was propped up by an assortment of colourful pillows and cushions against her bright red headboard which was in the shape of two luscious lips. Her mobile was trapped between her shoulder and ear as she painted on the finishing touches to her toenails which were strategically held apart by cotton wool padding.

"Still can't get a hold of him," she lied to Janice. The truth was that she was now playing hardball, waiting for Mick to call her after their recent, less than memorable night together. Although she was losing money in the short term she knew from previous experiences that it wouldn't be for too much longer and that she'd soon be reaping the benefits. She couldn't believe how drunk she'd gotten and began to question whether there was any date rape drug involved but soon dismissed the idea. Although her top and bra had been removed, the bottom half of her clothing had remained untouched and there were no signs of interference. It was as if her boss had started something but then had second thoughts. What puzzled her the most was that she half remembered talking to some nice chap, even if he was a bit different and then getting into a taxi with him. But for the life of her she had no idea how she ended up in bed with Mick above her place of work. She'd legged it as soon as she'd woken, not out of shame but just sheer disappointment that she'd jeopardised months of groundwork. She was no angel, having often snared strapping young lads who were well-on so that they could scratch an itch she just couldn't reach. Sometimes they weren't the hard men that they thought they were and she'd have to give them a Viagra just to get a jump start. Without exception they had always fled the following morning, mortified or perhaps fearful of the consequences of their actions.

"I need the money too, love, you try staying in three nights on the trot," she lied again to Janice.

Her colleague couldn't recall the last time she was out, never mind on three consecutive nights.

"I'm sorry for callin' ye, Tina but I just thought ye migh' have heard somethin' by now," Janice explained. Her two kids, Jack and Emma snuggled in a little closer, partly out of affection but mostly out of the need to stay warm. With no money to heat the flat, sharing a warm duvet was the best she could offer them at present.

The phone rang out again. Tina had lost patience waiting for her boss to call her and try as she might it was now getting the better of her. 'How dare that fucker take her for a ride,' she thought, 'As if she was some sort of cheap slapper. No, it was time to up the ante and to put the shyster on the back-foot.'

The taxi deposited Tina directly outside Flynn's Mini-Mart before spinning off in search of a new fare. She stood on the footpath staring up at the solitary light which was on in the upstairs flat. Knowing that Mick was at home and hadn't the courtesy to pick up her calls had only infuriated her even more, if that was possible. Having been unable to gain entry through the front on her last, sober visit, she strode around to the side and loudly bashed on the door with the heel of her hand. She took a step back as she readied herself for war. Nothing happened. She hammered on the door once again as well as giving it a kick for good measure even though she was careful not to damage her stylish and expensive footwear. There was still no reply. In the room above, Mick and Patrick could also hear the banging down below. The shopkeeper rose unsteadily from his armchair after almost consuming his entire bodyweight in wine. He clumsily tried to gather the curtains between his thumb and index finger but failed miserably.

"Somebody's knockin' for Billy no mates, wha'," Patrick couldn't help himself from saying.

Mick turned and gave him an ugly scowl before looking away. He roughly grabbed a handful of the curtains and tugged them back slightly without finesse, trying to see who was making all the racket. Tina stood on the pavement below with arms folded high across her chest, her annoyance at being ignored plain to see. This was definitely new territory. She contemplated finding something to put through the window but that was a tad excessive, for the moment at least. A thought popped into her head. What if something had happened to her boss and he was lying on the floor unconscious or even worse, how would she get her money out of him then? She made an executive decision and decided to get the law involved. If Mick was badly hurt then that would make complete sense as to why he was ignoring her and if there was nothing wrong with him then maybe it would do no harm to put the frighteners on. After all, he'd taken advantage of her while she was intoxicated and that was surely worth a serious amount of shillings. She turned her back on the shop, retrieved her mobile from her designer bag and dialled. Mick swayed slightly as he watched her through the slim parting in the curtains. An image of him lying on top of her popped into his head which was immediately followed by a wave of guilt washing over him. Something inside his head was trying to warn him that he could be in some serious trouble. Tina removed her phone from her ear and stared at the screen. Low battery. "For fuck's sake," she loudly swore, dumping the useless contraption back into her handbag. The bloke in the local phone shop was definitely going to get an earful after swearing that the expensive device which he'd recently sold her was the best on the market. He'd conveniently forgotten to mention that the battery was utter crap and that you'd want to have it recharging morning, noon and night. The fucking liar. In the near distance she could see a light above a vacant taxi cruising towards her. She quickly flagged it down and hopped into the back.

"Nearest Garda station," she instructed in a no nonsense tone.

As soon as the cab had disappeared from view Mick staggered over to Patrick and clipped him across the side of his head without uttering a single word.

Such was Tina's urgency to get inside the police station that she almost collided with a couple who were on their way out. She was about to berate the pair but noticed their obvious distress and decided to give them a pass. Billy's parents, Tony and Jackie had reported that their son had gone missing and they were desperately worried about him especially in light of the recent revelations with regards to who his real mother and father were. They hadn't mentioned their suspicions that their son was running errands for a high profile gangster and hoped that that was just hearsay. The older, more experienced Garda who dealt with them was very polite and understanding and promised to keep an eye out for him. He also had to inform them that because Billy was an adult and was only missing for a short space of time that there was very little else that he could do at this stage.

The flustered young Garda on duty had no doubt wished he was somewhere else, anywhere else rather than having to listen to Tina give him both barrels. Try as he might he couldn't get through to her that although they were taking her query seriously, resources were limited and at present it wasn't a priority. The older Garda came out from the back office to rescue his colleague. His face was etched in deep fissures carved out of years of experience.

The younger man was delighted to see him and said, "I've already explained numerous times to the girl..."

"Woman," Tina defiantly interjected.

The young policeman took a deep breath before slowly exhaling.

"The young woman, that there's nothing we can do..." he began.

Tina smacked her painted lips and said, "You could break down the bleeding door for starters."

"Everyone needs to calm down now..." the more experienced man said.

"I'm not..." Tina interrupted before being silence by the older Garda, holding up his shovel sized hand.

He turned to his colleague and said, "Get yourself a cuppa, I'll look after this."

"Appreciate that," the younger chap said and quickly disappeared not bothering to make eye contact with the clearly deranged woman.

"He hasn't a clue," commented Tina while shaking her head.

"That's enough," said the lawman in a firm tone leaving no doubt as to who was in charge, "Now, as my colleague has already informed you, we're extremely busy and there's more than likely some sort of simple explanation."

Tina wasn't going to be put off so easily. She rested her arms on the counter and leaned forward.

"I'm the shop manager," she explained, "And the boss said nothing to me about closing up. Besides, he owes me a week's wages."

The Garda didn't look convinced so Tina changed tact. Her expression softened and she fluttered her long eyelashes while giving her best innocent smile. Of course it had the desired effect.

"Look, I'll get one of our units to drop by when they get a chance…" the Garda said.

Tina playfully swept a piece of imaginary hair away from her face and said, "Promise?"

The Garda gave her a reassuring smile. "I promise," he replied.

The television screen indicated that the time was now 23.30pm but more importantly it was signalling that the lottery jackpot had been won with the winning ticket coming from Dublin. Patrick was oblivious to the update having fallen into a deep slumber despite his uncomfortable restraints. His mother used to always joke that he could sleep on a gymnast's beam. In the armchair close by Mick yawned loudly having only just woken from his drink induced sleep. He tried to stretch his bare arms towards the ceiling in an attempt to fire up his muscles but only got so far before letting them flop down again. His head lolled sideways allowing him to view the television without exerting himself. The message on screen finally registered and he gave his eyes a rub just to make sure he wasn't seeing things. As he unsteadily rose to his feet a darting pain shot across his temple and he immediately regretted being such a lush and sinking so many bottles of cheap vino. He stumbled slightly as he made his way over to Patrick who was peacefully snoring. He bent down next to his prisoner's ear.

"Halfway there," he shouted.

Patrick woke with a start. It took him a few moments to get his bearings and to remember how much peril he was in.

"Just thought you'd like to be kept up to speed," Mick said, nodding towards the television. Patrick glanced towards the screen and could see that the jackpot had been won.

His captor slumped down at the table where the pile of lotto slips sat, waiting to be checked.

"Right, better get to work," he said, picking up the pen and ruler.

Although Patrick felt a sense of great excitement that the winning ticket was most probably hidden in the paper heap he kept his feelings to himself. Mick had been very unkind to him but he still hoped that when the money was won that the shopkeeper would have a change of heart and agree to give him a decent share if not the fifty percent he truly deserved.

"Why don't ye just feed them into the machine?" he naively suggested.

Mick looked up from the Lotto slips with an expression he reserved for simpletons.

"What, check ten thousand euro worth of tickets? Do you not think that the lottery people would get suspicious?" he sarcastically asked.

"Didn't think but I suppose yer righ'," Patrick replied.

The smell of cigar smoke wafting through the room transported Patrick back to his younger, schoolboy days, watching his hero Clint Eastwood on screen playing the teak tough cowboy in The Outlaw Josey Wales. He hadn't been allowed to watch the film but that didn't stop him from sneaking out of bed in the middle of the night and sticking it on the video player. Some children kept a teddy bear for comfort whereas he had a collection of tapes which he brought with him every time he was passed on from one foster family to another. The rustling of paper close by interrupted his memory and brought him back to the present. He looked across at Mick, a lit cigar hanging rebelliously from his lip. The shopkeeper was meticulously checking ticket after ticket by drawing a line through the unsuccessful combinations of numbers. He didn't seem to care whether they were a match three, four or five, it had to be all six or nothing. Another lotto slip was ruled out and Mick folded it into a miniature paper aeroplane. He lit the end of it with his cigar and launched it towards Patrick who instinctively tilted his head sideways to avoid being hit. The aircraft was heading for a sizeable pile of losing tickets mangled at the base of a wall when it was caught by an invisible draft and it veered a few feet harmlessly to the left. "Another one goes down in flames," said the shopkeeper with no great surprise in his tone.

'This bloke's a bleedin' fruitcake,' Patrick thought but kept it to himself

"There's something I've been meaning to ask you," the shopkeeper began before biting off a piece of his cigar and spitting it onto the floor, "Why the obsession with money?"

"Long story," Patrick answered dismissively.

Mick raised an eyebrow and said, "Well it's not as if we're going anywhere anytime soon now, is it?"

The prisoner sighed before deciding to open up.

"Fast cars. That and I wanted to be someone, to belong somewhere, ye know," he said.

The shopkeeper didn't know but was curious none the less.

179

"Continue," he said.

"It's just that no matter wha' way I turn, cash or the lack of it keeps trippin' me up," Patrick honestly explained.

"And you really think that money's going to solve all of your problems?"asked the shopkeeper.

"Yeah," Patrick said, getting a bit more animated. "When you've got it, wha' ye say matters. People want to know ye, be around ye, love ye."

Mick guffawed at this last suggestion.

"You think that money can buy you love?" he asked.

"Definitely. When I was nine, me Ma was told she had cancer. There was talk of a possible cure in America but she hadn't the cash to go," Patrick explained. He closed his eyes and bowed his head slightly and said, "It was then that she decided to kill me."

The shopkeeper burst out laughing and said, "What a charming woman."

"No, ye don't understand," said Patrick, anxious to defend his mother's memory. "She didn't want me to be an orphan, to be sent to one of those bad homes so she gave me some sleepin' tablets, sealed up the flat and gassed us."

"And yet somehow, miraculously, you're still here?" Mick said, pointing out the obvious, "Tormenting decent law abiding citizens like my good self."

Patrick missed the shopkeeper's dig.

"Ye see the only problem was that me Ma was in arrears with the gas company and they came out to cut us off," he said.

"I don't believe it," Mick just about managed to say before laughing again and getting a fit of coughing midway through.

Patrick was determined to finish his story.

"Anyway, the gasman gets a smell while climbing the stairwell and calls the guards. The door got kicked in and apparently they found me and the Ma conked out on the sofa. I was put into care and me Ma got locked up and died a few weeks later. Ye see, she couldn't even afford the ultimate act of love."

A solitary tear escaped from Patrick's eye as he tried to hold it all together.

"They should have named you Oscar," laughed Mick, "With a performance like that."

The prisoner was more than a little taken aback by the shopkeeper's lack of empathy.

"I'm very surprised with yer attitude," he said, "Ye know wha' it's like growin' up under someone else's roof where ye can't afford to make mistakes, bein' constantly put down and told yer a loser."

Mick waved his hand dismissively.

"Pardon moi," he said. "That business I told you earlier about being adopted by my uncle was a load of horseshit. I was playing the sympathy card just to get round you." He laughed again and said, "You were right about my father giving me the shop though but not for my birthday, he left it to me in his will. Took him long enough to pop his clogs, the miserable old bastard." He looked wistfully into the distance. "Needed a helping hand in the finish as it happened." He glanced over at his prisoner and gave a haughty wink as if to say 'You'd have done the very same thing if you'd been in my shoes.'

Whatever chances Patrick had of getting out of this thing alive were rapidly shrinking by the hour.

Patrick didn't open his mouth again despite Mick taking the piss out of him on several occasions. The shopkeeper had eventually given up taunting his victim and got down to finishing his task of manually checking every single lotto slip. Eventually, at four a.m. the job was completed. Mick scrunched up the last ticket and hopped it off of his prisoner's head.

"Looks like your master plan has failed," he said spitefully.

Patrick really thought it was going to work. He gave the shopkeeper a contemptuous look but remained tight lipped which only infuriated Mick even further. The shopkeeper couldn't control his temper and grabbed Patrick roughly by the shirt, shaking him violently. He then stopped all of a sudden, a confused look sweeping across his face. He reached inside his prisoner's shirt pocket and pulled out another lottery ticket.

"What's this then, have you been holding out on me?" he asked with genuine surprise.

Patrick had forgotten all about the lotto slip which he'd bought after depositing the money in the bank a few days previously.

Mick scrutinised the ticket, reading the numbers aloud and ever so slowly, "Two, thirteen, fifteen, nineteen, twenty-five, twenty-six, I don't believe it."

Incredible as it seemed Patrick had indeed won the national lottery. The stunned shopkeeper stood still for a few seconds trying to comprehend what he'd just read. Elated, he suddenly began to skip round the room singing in a child-like voice, "Cause I've got the golden ticket, yes I've got the golden ticket. La la la la la la..."

"Ye mean we won, we really did it?" Patrick asked, not believing his own words. Although he always felt that it was his destiny, if he was being honest with himself there were times when he'd had serious doubts.

Mick stopped his prancing and arched an eyebrow at his prisoner. He sauntered over to him, hunched down and placed his hands on his thighs. "What's this we?" he said.

"I know we've had our differences but I presume that we're still goin' to split it fifty-fifty?" Patrick said.

"Not on your life," answered Mick. "I'm keeping the lot and we'll call it compensation for all the trouble you've caused me."

Halfway through the night shift the older Garda was bleary-eyed filling out forms at the front desk when he heard distant singing growing closer. He glanced up and spotted one of their regulars who was in fine fettle being escorted through the station double doors by two uniformed officers.

"Bad boys, bad boys, what ye gonna do, what ye gonna do when they come for you," sang the drunk.

"There you are, Larry," the older Garda said kindly.

"Come on, time for bed," the female guard wearily said as she gently steered the drunken man down the corridor which led to a small number of holding cells.

Larry stopped dead in his tracks, stared at his escort, looking offended.

"I'll have you know that I'm a happily married man," he pointed out.

The older Garda smiled and said, "I thought she left you years ago?"

"She did and that's why I'm happily married. Boom, boom," replied Larry, bursting into laughter and taking absolutely no offence.

He then carried on with his singing, "I shot the sheriff but I did not shoot the dep u ty..."

He was led away with the second Garda bringing up the rear. The young policeman from earlier popped his head out from a room behind the front desk.

"Milk, no sugar," he said, handing over a freshly brewed coffee.

"Good man," said the more experienced Garda, tasting his beverage and giving a satisfied nod, "We might keep you yet."

The younger man smiled. "What's all the commotion about?" he asked.

"Ah, it's only one of our regulars, Larry. A harmless aul soul," his colleague explained. "Hard to believe that he was once a multi-millionaire."

"Yeah?" said the curious young Garda.

"Made a fortune from the driving school game as well as the limo business."

"So what went wrong?"

The older Garda shrugged his shoulders and said, "God only knows. There were lots of rumours flying around at the time but I never took much heed of them."

"Meant to ask you, how did you get rid of the mad woman who was in earlier looking for her missing boss?"

The experienced policeman immediately set his cup down and said, "Jesus, I forgot all about her. Mind the desk for a tick."

It was the quietest time of the night for the two patrolmen as they cruised along the deserted streets. All the pub and nightclub gang were gone home if they were any bit sensible and it was still a little too early for the drug addicts in desperate need of a fix to begin their daily hunt.

"Any units near the North Circular Road, St. Peter's Church area, over?" asked a tired voice on the police radio. One of the uniformed guards, a foxy headed fella named Connie, picked up the receiver.

"Twenty-two here, go ahead," he said, trying to suppress a yawn.

"Need you to take a look at a premises…" the controller said before being interrupted by static.

"Repeat, over," said Connie.

More static followed before the voice back at the control centre could be properly heard.

"Flynn's Mini-Mart. There's growing concern with regards to the owner's whereabouts, over."

The patrol car eased to a halt outside Flynn's shop. The two policemen had already spotted the light on in the upstairs flat on their approach. They exchanged looks and nodded as if to say 'a complete waste of time'. Foxy took his cap from the dashboard and opened the car door. His colleague in the passenger seat made to do the same but Foxy shook his head.

"Stay there, this won't take long," he said.

"Need to stretch the legs," replied his colleague, "Doesn't help being six-foot four and stuck in this thing for hours on end."

Unaware that he had visitors below, Mick was busy reading the instructions on a brown cylinder containing sleeping pills. He popped four out onto the palm of his hand before rolling his tongue round the inside of his mouth and deciding to add another four.

The side passage was unlit so the tall Garda had to use his powerful torch to illuminate the way. His colleague strolled up to the front door and spotted the sign in the window indicating as to why the shop was closed. In the upstairs flat

Mick was now standing over Patrick with a glass of water held in one hand and the bundle of tablets in the other.

"I don't want you conscious while you're being dismembered, couldn't deal with all that unnecessary screaming," Mick bluntly informed his prisoner.

A loud banging on the side door caused him to jump slightly, spilling some of the water and dropping the tablets onto the floor. He turned his head and listened carefully. Moments later there was another round of even more fervent banging. Patrick glanced frantically in the direction of the door, praying that someone was going to come charging up the stairs and rescue him just in the nick of time. He thought about shouting for help but feared the repercussions if he wasn't heard.

"Hello, is there anyone home? It's the Gardai," shouted the tall lawman through the letterbox.

"That's all I fucking need," said Mick. He dropped to his knees and hurriedly began to gather up the fallen pills and shove them back into the container.

There was more insistent knocking and the shopkeeper guessed that he didn't have much time before a size twelve boot was put through the door. He got to his feet and glanced over at the role of tape then back at Patrick. Deciding that he really didn't have the time to gag his prisoner he instead put a finger to his lips before running it across his throat in a mock slicing action. "Try anything and there'll be no pain relief," he warned.

Foxy joined his colleague at the side door and gave him a questioning look. The taller man straightened up and shrugged his shoulders.

"There's no answer," he said, "And I'm almost after taking it off the hinges."

Foxy removed his cap and scratched his scalp.

"What d'you think, will we call for backup?" he suggested.

"Wouldn't bother, we'll be only waiting around all night," said his colleague.

Both men eyed up the door.

"You better kick it in so," said Foxy, "I've a county final next weekend."

The taller man grinned at his partner. He removed his cap, handed it to him and took several steps backwards.

The shopkeeper stood at the top of the stairs and shouted, "Hold your horses." He spun his head to the side, looking through the open door to where Patrick sat tied to the chair, smiling like an angel. Satisfied, Mick started to descend the steps. "I'm coming," he shouted.

No sooner was the shopkeeper out of sight when Patrick began to shuffle and wobble his chair forward towards the kitchen table where Jaws lay speared. It was a lot more difficult than he first anticipated but once he found his rhythm he began to make real progress. He knew it was now or never as he stretched his neck awkwardly trying to reach the knife. Outside, the foxy headed Garda held up a hand to halt his colleague's imminent charge. Mick glanced back up the stairs, listening carefully but could hear nothing. Patrick stretched his neck a little further and tried to grip the knife with his teeth without slicing open his mouth. It took him a couple of go's to pull the stubborn knife out of the wooden table. He then carefully used the side of the table to slide Jaws along the blade and off onto the floor leaving a trail of blood smeared on the cold steel.

Mick was now at the bottom of the stairs leaning his head slightly towards the closed door. The letterbox was suddenly pushed open causing him to immediately jump back.

"Mick Flynn?" Foxy asked in a gruff, business-like manner.

"Yes," the shopkeeper tentatively answered.

"Garda Ryan and Garda Mullins here, could you please open up?" said Foxy.

Mullins, the taller policeman took his cap back from his colleague and placed it on top of his head.

"Shit, shit, shit," Mick said in a low voice while tugging at his butchered beard.

"Are you still there?" Garda Ryan asked.

"What do you want?" said Mick.

Garda Ryan looked at his colleague, threw his eyes to the heavens before continuing.

"Just a quick word, to see if you're okay?" he said.

In the upstairs flat Patrick was busily sawing the blade through the rope restraints although he felt he was getting nowhere. 'Like usin' a poxy butter knife,' he thought to himself. He wasn't quite sure if it really was the Gardai at the door below but he remembered a phrase he'd once heard at school many moons ago. 'Be an active participant in your own rescue.' Well right now he was doing all that and some.

"I'm fine, night so," Mick said to the letterbox.

Garda Ryan was starting to get annoyed.

"Mr. Flynn, I need you to open the door right now," he sternly said. "It won't take long, I promise."

"Okay, okay. Give me a minute," the shopkeeper reluctantly replied. He exhaled loudly then took the stairs two at a time.

Patrick was finally free of his restraints but he could hear Mick bounding up the stairs. He righted the chair and quickly sat back in place, snatching the lengths of rope off of the floor and throwing them over himself. The shopkeeper was just outside the room when Patrick spotted the bloodied carcass of his fish abandoned on the ground. He didn't waste time. He extended his leg and promptly kicked Jaws across the floor and out of sight.

"Sorry, bud," he quietly apologised.

He'd no sooner gotten rid of the evidence when Mick stuck his big head inside the room, hurriedly checking that everything was okay. Patrick stared at the ground not wanting to give the game away. Satisfied, the shopkeeper disappeared again and headed for his bedroom. Patrick knew that this was probably going to be his one and only chance. He jumped up, grabbed the CCTV disc off the mantelpiece and stuffed it down his pants. He then peeked through the sliver of a crack between the door and the frame. Mick was nowhere to be seen. Stealthily, he made his way down the stairs in his bid to escape. About midway down he stepped onto the creaking timber once again. He immediately lifted his foot, silently cursing his sloppiness. He was about to descend the rest of the way when he remembered that the winning lottery ticket was still sitting on top of the mantelpiece. The bottom of the stairs and his freedom were a mere few steps away while a scrap of paper worth millions was going a begging. He broke free from the pull of reason and nipped back upstairs to claim his rightful prize.

The straps of the dress were hastily pulled back up on Mick's shoulders. He reefed open several closet doors and hurriedly searched through the items of clothing hanging from an aluminium rail. He finally settled on the fluffy housecoat with the Disney motif on the breast pocket. It was an apparently innocent gift from his ex but he'd known in his heart that the scheming bitch was dropping subliminal hints, trying to blag a trip to Florida or Paris at the very least.

The winning lottery ticket was like a glorious beacon, drawing Patrick towards it. He darted across the room without making a sound and snatched the slip before dashing back out again. Unfortunately in all of his excitement he forgot to check to see if the coast was clear and crashed straight into Mick who was doing up the belt on his housecoat. The pair collided. Patrick lost his footing and to his horror went tumbling down the stairs, careering headfirst into the wall at the bottom. There was no movement. Blood began to pool on the floor around his skull. His captor stood on the landing looking down, his mouth agape, not really believing what was happening. He was quickly brought back to the here and now when the side door was loudly hammered.

"Is everything alright in there?" Foxy urgently called through the letterbox.

Images of some prison cell with an assortment of sleazy characters was enough to get Mick going. He ran down the stairs, grabbed Patrick off the ground as if he weighed nothing and flung him over his beefy shoulder.

"Yes, hold on," he shouted back to the policemen outside.

He then proceeded to hurriedly climb the stairs like a man possessed, reaching the spare room where he dumped Patrick's unconscious body onto the bed. He raced back downstairs and paused for a moment to collect his thoughts and slow down his breathing. Finally, he was ready to answer the door. He opened it slightly, taking in the faces of the two concerned Gardai outside.

"Sorry for calling so late and obviously getting you out of bed," Foxy said, trying to suss things out as discreetly as possible, "But we just wanted to make sure that everything was okay?"

"I told you, it is," Mick curtly replied.

Foxy's colleague smiled broadly and said, "We can see that now, it's just that one of your staff was a small bit concerned as to your whereabouts."

"Well as you can see, I'm clearly here. I'll ring them tomorrow, I just forgot to explain."

"An easy thing to happen under the circumstances," Foxy said kindly.

The shopkeeper was puzzled.

Foxy shuffled uneasily, unable to maintain eye contact. "Are they dead?" he asked.

Mick's heart skipped a beat. Had they seen his prisoner catapult down the stairs?

"What?" he feebly managed to ask.

Garda Ryan glanced at his colleague hoping for support.

Garda Mullins cleared his throat and said, "Your relative? The sign in the window?"

Mick held onto the door for fear of falling over with the relief.

"Look, we know it can be hard to accept the loss of a loved one so if you need someone to talk to..." Garda Ryan gently said.

"Everyone's doing okay and I don't need to speak to anyone," the shopkeeper insisted.

Garda Ryan gave a sympathetic nod and said, "Okay, Mick. We'd still like to take a quick look round, our superiors would give us an earful if we didn't."

Mick resigned himself to the fact that the only way he was going to get rid of these two boyos was to let them in.

"You better make it quick," he said making no attempt to hide his annoyance.

"It's just routine," Garda Ryan replied.

The shopkeeper allowed the policemen to enter, ushering them along the corridor. While doing his best to shield the blood from Patrick's head wound, which had formed a sizeable puddle on the floor, he accidentally stepped back into it.

"This way?" asked Garda Mullins.

"Eh, straight ahead and through that door," Mick said, pointing the way.

Mullins discreetly poked his colleague in the side and nodded towards the crates of milk and bundles of newspapers lined up along one wall.

Foxy paused and looked at the shopkeeper.

"Are you sure you wouldn't like to chat to someone?" he asked.

"I'm positive," Mick replied. His patience was being severely tested by the pair. He walked forward not realising that he was now leaving a trail of bloody footprints in his wake.

"Through there," he said, motioning for them to move forward and practically shoving them through the door.

The officers entered the room, immediately scanning the place for evidence. Mick rested against the doorframe and watched the expressions on their faces. He knew that they'd be thinking he took no pride in his shop and that really bugged him. That little fucker upstairs had wrecked the place but karma was now paying him a well deserved return visit. The two guards strolled up and down the aisles and although the place was in a mess the owner wasn't making any complaints and he seemed to be physically okay despite his unusual facial hair.

Garda Mullins looked Mick square in the eyes.

"One last chance. Are you sure you wouldn't like us to call someone to help you out?" he asked.

The shopkeeper smiled but didn't answer. He turned round to lead the policemen back down the hallway and out the side door when his heart plummeted. There, as plain as day, was a trail of bloody footprints.

"Is everything okay?" Mullins asked, noticing the shopkeeper's body stiffen.

"Yes," Mick barely replied. He then slapped the side of his head and spun round to face the guards. "What am I thinking of," he said, "Here we are skulking around like criminals. Come on and I'll let you out the front door."

The shopkeeper's heart thumped violently but he did his best to appear calm while ushering the officers outside. The young men opened the doors to their squad car and reluctantly prepared to leave. There was something not quite right about the situation but they'd done their job. Mick put on a beaming smile while giving an enthusiastic wave hoping that they'd just get the hint and clear the hell off. He was unaware however that his robe had become undone revealing the red dress which he was wearing underneath. Garda Mullins couldn't help but glance over at his colleague. Foxy's eyes flashed with devilment while the corners of his mouth turned upwards. The shopkeeper was puzzled until he realised that his robe was wide open for all to see. He hastily gathered the ends of the belt trying to hide his modesty. Although unprofessional, the two young men were struggling to hold in the laughter. They jumped into their car and quickly drove off before it got them into more trouble back at the station.

"That fecking bastard," Mick cursed, his cheeks reddening with an equal measure of both anger and embarrassment. It was bad enough that his shop had been ransacked but to now have the local police force think that he was gay was worst again. He couldn't think of anything more revolting. Once he'd retreated into the safety of his shop he slammed the door shut almost shattering the glass. If that fucker upstairs wasn't already dead he was definitely going to finish him off.

Chapter 12

Sunday evening.

Patrick hadn't in fact died in the fall but he'd come pretty close. The bleeding to his head had eventually stopped after a couple of hours no thanks to Mick. The shopkeeper had calmed since the previous night and had convinced himself that once he was seen with a gorgeous woman on his arm, any rumours which the two guards might put out about his sexuality would be soon put to bed. Determined that there weren't going to be any more daring escapes and near misses, he fixed a thin rope across the stairs at the midway point, down at foot level. He plucked the rope to make sure it was taut enough for the task he had in mind. Satisfied, he glanced back up the stairs and grinned.

"Just in case, my slippery friend, just in case," he whispered aloud.

Wet stains covered the chest area of Patrick's sweatshirt where Mick had force fed him the sleeping pills, washed down by copious amounts of water. The process had reminded Mick of a water-boarding scene he'd watched during some war film a while back and he had often wondered about its effectiveness. He didn't need to wonder any longer having seen firsthand how his prisoner had gasped and struggled wildly, the fear of drowning very evident in his eyes. Mick felt no remorse for doing what he'd done and excused himself with the fact that it would have all been avoidable had this man not kidnapped him to begin with. Patrick tried to focus on the shopkeeper as he busily passed back and forth, carrying various items of clothing and stuffing them into a suitcase. He tried to say something to his captor but he was only talking gibberish as the drugs took hold. No matter how hard he tried to keep his eyes open, he just couldn't. His eyelids kept sliding shut, demanding sleep only for his head to loll forward and startle him awake once again.

Mick stopped midstride and looked at his pitiful prisoner.

"There's no point trying to fight it," he smugly said, "I've given you enough tablets to knock out an elephant, well a small one at the very least."

The shopkeeper piled the last of his clothes into the jaded suitcase and closed over the lid but despite his best efforts the teeth of the giant zips wouldn't bite together. He hadn't the time to go through his stuff and discard the surplus so he decided instead to sit on the case and force it shut, hoping that the seams would hold. After a small bit of brute force the job was done. He hunched down in front of his prisoner.

"You didn't think that I was actually going to cut you up into little pieces like some sort of savage now, did you?" he said.

Drool escaped from the corner of Patrick's slanted mouth which now resembled an ocean liner badly listing as it prepared to slip beneath the surface to its watery doom. The shopkeeper got to his feet and slipped on his jacket.

He tapped the inside breast pocket and reassuringly felt his passport and wallet. The winning lotto ticket was whipped off the mantelpiece, the stuffed suitcase was collected and he was on his way to sunnier climes.

"I've cancelled the deliveries even though that donkey of a milkman should have known better and I've tied up a few other loose ends so there's no reason for anyone to disturb your sleep," he gleeful said, heading for the door.

Patrick's eyes shot open in one last futile attempt to stay awake.

The shopkeeper shook his head and said, "And as for your not so good self. As soon as I'm safely away I'll call the Guards and have them free you if you're still alive and kicking that is. I've even written a short note exonerating you of any wrong doing, after all, who am I to hold a grudge against a man for committing a spot of kidnapping, burglary and assault."

Patrick finally succumbed to sleep. The shopkeeper began to whistle Money, Money, Money as he pinned the handwritten note to his prisoner's chest. He then flicked his chubby index finger forcefully against Patrick's cheek but there was no response.

Mick paused at the top of the stairs still not believing that the simpleton in the adjoining room had the where with all to conjure up such a basic yet ingenious plan. The lottery win would destroy a commoner like Patrick who wasn't used to handling large sums of money and Mick firmly believed that he was actually doing him a favour. He waltzed down the stairs, the winning ticket in one hand and his case, which no longer felt in the least bit heavy, in the other. His mind began to wander to some exotic place where a topless Tina was straddling him on a bed dressed with gleaming white linen sheets while flimsy curtains gently fluttered in the background against an azure blue sky. Tina was sensually rubbing oil into his bare chest using her ample breasts and working her way lower towards his erect manhood. He couldn't help but smile at the thought and gave the winning ticket a kiss for good luck. It was at that precise moment that his foot got caught on a different sort of booby-trap altogether. The tripwire! By the time he realised what was happening it was already too late. His hefty bulk was thrown forward, his face screwed up in horror. The suitcase was flung ahead of him, almost spinning in slow motion. Whether it was by instinct or just sheer stubbornness Mick held onto the lottery ticket for dear life. He wanted to scream but his voice-box failed to muster a single sound. The case smashed against the wall at the bottom of the stairs and seemed to groan as the seams finally gave way and the clothes inside burst free. A sickening thump followed, accompanied by the unmistakable crunch of bones as the shopkeeper ploughed into the painted concrete wall. His head was twisted in an unnatural angle to his lifeless body with the lotto ticket still clutched tightly in his outstretched hand. A hint of blood appeared at the entrance to both his nostrils and at one ear but other than that there was absolutely no other movement at all.

Janice had fortuitously bumped into Tina in the shopping centre earlier that day and had learned that Mick had been in contact and had promised her a tasty redundancy package. Needless to say, Janice was absolutely livid. She'd found it very hard to comprehend at first but Tina was spending all round her and was laden down with several new outfits for a little foreign holiday that their boss was also taking her on. And if it was true why would Mick treat her in such a disrespectful manner after all her years of loyal service? She'd never been late and was very seldom absent despite the crap going on in her life with her late husband and then to be treated like this? She wasn't having it. She was going round to the shop to demand answers.

Ignoring the front of the mini-mart, Janice made a beeline for the side-door. She reefed a set of keys from her jacket pocket catching them on a loose piece of thread. She'd meant to nip the thread and re-stitch it on a number of occasions but had somehow never gotten round to it. Her children always seemed to distract her. Such was her anger she'd didn't care how much damage she did to her jacket and tore the keys free. She unlocked the door and shoved it open but it only moved a matter of inches before the obstruction on the other side halted her progress. Not one to be deterred so easily she adjusted her stance, dropped her shoulder and pushed against the door with all of her might. After a tremendous amount of effort the door eventually shifted just enough for her to squeeze through. Not being able to fully see where she was going she inadvertently stepped into a gap between the shopkeeper's bent elbow and his prone torso. When she moved again her foot got caught and she stumbled forwards. She was unable to correct her fall and landed directly on top of Mick, her face coming within inches of his. She shrieked and instinctively shoved both her hands against the deathly corpse, rolling sideways while springing to her feet and quickly retreating to the relative safety of the wall behind her. Her chest was thumping wildly as her mind raced through all the possible scenarios. It took her a few minutes to calm the rhythm of her heartbeat to something resembling normal. She knew just by looking at her boss that he was dead, really dead. The pallor of his skin was a giveaway as was his unnaturally twisted head. It looked as if he'd fallen down the stairs while carrying the case, a tragic accident. She shot a glance up the stairs believing she'd heard a noise and listened carefully. There were no further sounds. While it was probably just her imagination she inexplicably felt the need to investigate things further. Using the walls as a guide she shuffled her way around Mick's corpse, doing her best not to look at him. She then began to tentatively climb the stairs one slow step at a time while staring straight ahead ready to take flight if someone happened to pounce. One of the timbers groaned loudly beneath her foot giving away any chance of a surprise 'attack'. She immediately lifted it and was puzzled to spot what appeared to be some sort of tripwire. A shiver ran down her spine causing the hairs on the back of her neck to stand on end. She seriously thought about turning round but despite her fears she was compelled to go on. Again, she listened intently but could only hear silence. This was absolutely insane. Her brain was screaming for her to get out of the building as quickly as possible but somehow her feet disobeyed and she inexplicably began to ascend.

The closed bathroom door was the first one that Janice went to. She stared hard at the brass, ball-type handle, her right hand subconsciously clenching and releasing at the thoughts of what lay beyond. She caught the handle and slowly turned it. Billy, the teenage thug who was now sporting a perfectly formed, circular bruise on his forehead from the earlier hammer blow, watched the brass ball as it was painstakingly turned anticlockwise. His luck was surely in and he was going to be rescued. He rocked violently back and forth on the toilet bowl where he was tightly bound, tearing his skin against his rope restraints but not caring in the least. That fruitcake of a shopkeeper wasn't going to be as lucky once he got free. He was going to give him a right few slaps before handing the slithery fuck over to his boss, Frank Harris. He was almost salivating at the thoughts of the untold violence that Harris would surely mete out. Maybe the gaffer would let him join in with the beating as well. That would be fucking awesome. The brass ball stopped and Billy prepared himself to meet his hero. Then a thought crossed his mind. What if the looper shopkeeper was returning to finish him off? The doorknob suddenly began to turn the opposite way. Confusion swept across his face, his brain struggling to comprehend what was going on. Outside, Janice had been distracted by something on the other side of the landing. She could make out through the partially opened door what appeared to be a man's legs fastened at the ankles and sitting on a chair. She left go of the door knob and inched forward towards the open doorway oblivious to Billy who was now going absolutely berserk inside the bathroom. With the tip of her foot Janice gently pushed the living-room door open the rest of the way.

Patrick was slumped in the chair with his head titled forwards and slightly to one side. Janice cautiously edged closer, terrified that this man was also dead. She was scared shitless that whoever had caused all of this mayhem was still lurking somewhere, preparing to leap out and to make her victim number three. She extended her shaking hand and placed two fingers on the bound man's neck checking for a pulse. After a bit of manoeuvring she found it, albeit a weak one. Miraculously he was still alive. She quickly took a step back surprised at the result but also very much relieved. She took several deep breathes, slowly exhaling each time. When she had gathered herself she leaned forward again and raised the man's chin. There was something very familiar about his face but she couldn't quite place it. And then it clicked. He was the lovely, kind chap who had come to her aid when she'd been brutally robbed in the cemetery by that scumbag. When she gently let his chin go she spotted the note stuck to his chest. She glanced round the room to make sure they were alone before unpinning the message and reading it.

"*To whom it may concern. I, Mick Flynn, the proprietor of this glorious emporium do hereby solemnly exonerate this man (please see man attached), Patrick something or other, from any wrong doing other than being a pain in the arse and being completely bonkers. Yours truly, Mick. P.S. Don't bother looking for me as I've just won the lottery and will be taking up residence in a palatial pile somewhere very far from here where there's no extradition, enjoying the finer things which life has to offer.*"

"The bastard," Janice exclaimed aloud, not that she was in the habit of cursing but here she was struggling to pay her debts while her boss had intended to just up and leave and swan around the world taking that floozy, Tina in tow. She suddenly felt a pang of guilt for speaking ill of the dead and couldn't help but give herself a quick blessing to balance the books so to speak. The note was gently pinned back onto Patrick's chest. She couldn't fathom for the life of her how he had ended up here, above the shop where she worked of all places and tied to a chair. At least he had survived. Despite the crap hand she'd been dealt with in life she was still a firm believer in the Almighty and maybe her coming here was an act of divine intervention for Patrick's earlier kindness. As she surveyed the rest of the room again, only this time in less of a panic, she noticed the huge pile of lottery slips discarded on the floor in the corner.

Curiosity got the better of her. She picked up a few of the tickets and noted the lines drawn through the rows of numbers. It looked as if someone had painstakingly checked each and every one of them with a pen. The whole thing was absolutely bizarre. Surely it would have been a lot easier to have fed them into the machine and checked them that way? But then again why were there so many of them? For whatever reason, it looked as if her boss or former boss to be more precise had bizarrely printed them for himself.

After checking the shop and the downstairs backroom Janice returned to the body of the shopkeeper. Her eyes were drawn towards the winning lottery slip which she knew had to be worth at least several million euro. Just like with Charlie and Willy Wonka, this was her family's ticket out of poverty.

She reached out tentatively but pulled her hand back again, biting down hard on her lip. Eventually, she found the courage to pluck the ticket from Mick's stiff hand. There were no pen lines running through this slip unlike the discarded ones in the room above. Janice looked towards the exit then glanced back up the stairs. She'd never felt so conflicted in her life. She dropped to her knees and rummaged through Mick's jacket searching for his mobile phone. It was locked but that wasn't a problem. Her boss was constantly forgetting his pin and had asked her on numerous occasions to remind him. She quickly tapped in the code and dialled 112. The phone started to ring and was answered almost immediately by a firm but polite sounding woman in an anonymous call centre somewhere in Ireland who identified herself as Linda. Janice was just about to answer Linda's question when she noticed something peculiar in the bottom half of the phone screen. She brought it closer for inspection as the emergency operative on the other end of the line was repeating herself. Janice tapped on the icon and up popped a series of photos of a half naked woman, lying on a bed. Janice put a hand to her mouth when she realised that the woman in the photos was her colleague, Tina. The voice on the phone was growing more anxious and annoyed at the same time. Janice terminated the call.

"So this is what you have to do nowadays to get a promotion is it?" she said, angrily shaking her head. She knew her colleague was a schemer but she didn't think she'd stoop this low for a poxy promotion in a sweetshop. She looked from the phone to the winning lottery ticket then glanced up at the ceiling.

Chapter 13

The outside of the airport was a hive of activity with a constant flow of people being either dropped off or collected. Security personnel were kept on their toes moving on the chancers who were parked in the set-down only section waiting for loved ones to arrive rather than pay for the seriously overpriced parking. Inside the building things were also busy but in a more mannerly fashion as people were herded from one line to another, around a series of metal poles and tape. The recent chaotic scenes of travellers having to queue longer than their actual flight had been somewhat resolved. One queue was particularly long however with Tina positioned at the head of it. She was wearing a nice little summery number, nothing too revealing but enough to raise any red-blooded man's pulse a few notches. Her face was hidden behind sunglasses reminiscent of a Hollywood diva from the fifties and her hands were firmly planted on her hips. Her demeanour had tantrum written all over it.

"Well thanks for nothing, you fat cow," she swore at the flustered middle-aged woman cowering behind the desk. Tina snatched her magazine from the countertop, turned and grabbed the handle of her wheelie suitcase and stormed away. She didn't get very far before colliding with a man with beautifully bronzed skin who was dressed in a fitted pilot's uniform. Her magazine fell to the floor.

"Watch where you're fuc..." she said but never finished the sentence.

The pilot with the sultry looks and dazzling smile had picked up the magazine and was holding it out for her.

"Pardon moi, mademoiselle," he said, oozing sex.

Tina's cross face instantly switched to one of a 'coy damsel in distress.' She had it down to a fine art after years of experience. The sunglasses were slowly removed and she gently chewed on one of the arms of the frame while fluttering her extended eyelashes.

"Where is your lover?" the pilot asked, well used to playing the game himself and going straight for the jugular.

Tina twirled a strand of loose hair with a manicured nail and said, "I'm travelling alone, like to keep my options open."

The pilot flashed his killer smile and took hold of her suitcase.

"Let me," he said and held out his arm for her to link. "I'm on a layover."

Tina paused momentarily but only for dramatic effect. She accepted the handsome pilot's offer, linked arms and headed for the bar. When Mick showed up this would only help to increase the stakes and if for some reason he didn't appear then the trip to the airport wouldn't have been a complete waste of time after all.

Three weeks later...

A delivery man whistled cheerfully as he pushed his two wheeled hand-truck stacked high with cardboard boxes towards a Garda who was posted behind yellow crime scene tape. Close-by, a news reporter was busily fixing his thinning, fair hair while his cameraman waited impatiently, having already decided upon the ideal shot. Flynn's Mini-Mart was clearly captured in the background.

"I've a couple of packages need sorting out," the delivery chap cheerfully said to the Garda on sentry.

The policeman opened his mouth to reply only to be drowned out by a blast of a horn from an agitated van driver. The Garda smiled and waited for the noise to abate.

"You're not the only one," he eventually said, nodding towards the backed up line of courier vans, some of which had been abandoned.

The deliveryman glanced round and saw a number of unimpressed drivers walking towards the yellow tape, carrying an assortment of parcels. One lad was sweating profusely as he struggled with a new exercise bike. The delivery chap turned back to the Garda and gave him a look as if to say 'What the hell is going on?"

"We've a few packages of our own to sort out first," the policeman said, pointing to a couple of occupied body bags being wheeled out on trolleys by the side of Flynn's Mini-Mart. The immaculately dressed undertakers accompanying the corpses looked suitably sombre for the grave occasion, keenly aware of the presence of the television cameras. There was nothing like a potential murder case to showcase your business and there was definitely no such thing as bad publicity.

The Garda photographer had finished taking snaps of every inch of the inside of the shop and was packing away most of her expensive equipment. She'd spent years capturing the images of sickly thin models, some of whom might well have been dead with their brittle and pasty skin and protruding bones. The forensic team had gone through the place with a fine toothcomb having already dusted it for fingerprints. A familiar, stocky figure stood in the centre of the room surveying his surroundings. It was detective Murphy, the landlord's brother. He was scouting for clues using his years of experience and a well trained eye. The ceiling mounted camera caught his attention and he began to rapidly click his fingers at a young Garda in uniform who was standing nearby. The Garda obediently hurried towards him.

"I want to see what that camera picked up," Murphy ordered, pointing towards the ceiling, "And find out where the backup footage is kept. I want to know how far back it goes."

Debbie was sat at her little table in Flat 1B, chewing on her already decimated fingernails with Tommy standing just behind her. His hands were placed reassuringly on her shoulders.

"Where d'ye think he is now?" she asked, all concerned.

"Knowing Patrick, probably livin' it up somewhere exotic," replied Tommy.

They were staring at a pair of airline tickets lying on the table with an accompanying note on some fancy stationary with a pink floral border.

"Thanks for mindin' me stuff and for bein' great neighbours. Hope ye like the sun - Patrick."

The plane tickets were for Benidorm and the accompanying holiday brochure showed a nice looking hotel boasting three swimming pools and an all-inclusive food and drink package. Tommy leaned down lower and kissed his partner lovingly on the neck. She responded by turning her head round and planting her painted lips onto his. They were oblivious to the television which was on in the background showing the news. The stern newscaster was sat bolt upright in his chair, his hands resting on the desk in front of him with his bony fingers interlocked.

"We are now going over live to Colm Lacey, our reporter at the tragic scene," he said, swivelling his chair slightly to the left to face the monitor. The fair haired reporter appeared onscreen with his perfectly quaffed hair, standing bolt upright in front of Flynn's Mini-Mart.

"So, Colm, what's the latest on this unfolding drama?" the newscaster solemnly asked.

Colm brought the microphone close to his mouth trying to ignore the goofy smile on the delivery chap who was inching closer, trying to get into the shot for his fifteen seconds of fame.

"After preliminary examinations it appears that one of the men found earlier today died as a result of injuries sustained in a fall," he reported.

"Do we know the identities of any of the victims?" asked the newscaster.

"A spokesperson for An Garda Siochana said that they won't be releasing any of the names until the next of kin have been informed."

"Is it any clearer what actually happened and how the deceased lost their lives?" the newscaster asked.

"The Garda spokesperson refused to give any further details. Speculation is rife however that this could possibly be gang related but the Gardai would not be drawn on this. Another theory doing the rounds however is that the victim found at the base of the stairs was in fact the shop owner. It is believed that he was trying to make his escape after being held hostage for several days during a botched robbery."

The picture on screen returned to the studio where the suitably, serious faced newscaster was waiting.

"That was Colm Lacey reporting on the gruesome discoveries made earlier today at the 'Little Shop of Horrors' as some sections of the media are now dubbing it. In other news today..."

Delivering news of a loved one's passing, especially a young person, was a terrible thing to have to do under normal circumstances but it was way more tragic when the death was as a result of a crime and totally avoidable. The female garda who was tasked with the difficult job took her time and spoke softly and slowly to Billy's distraught parents, Jackie and Tony. She explained in minimal detail how Billy had been found in the bathroom above Flynn's Mini-Mart, tied and gagged before reassuring them that the Gardai were doing everything to apprehend the person or persons responsible for his untimely death.

The cemetery was dead quiet as Patrick stood in front of the newly erected black marble headstone with the ornate gold writing. It read: *Patrick Bridges Snr & Maggie Bridges. Dearly missed by your loving son, Patrick.* He resembled an extra from a big budget mafia film dressed in his stylish and tailor fitted navy suit with a pale blue silk handkerchief poking out from the top pocket. A designer pair of sunglasses completed the look. He removed the handkerchief, leaned forward and carefully wiped clean a trace of dirt only he could see from the writing on the headstone.

"Gotta go, me pal's waitin' for me," he said and turned to walk away. After taking several steps he paused and glanced back over his shoulder. "And tell the main man thanks again for sortin' me out."

Patrick strolled towards the cemetery car park where a solitary vehicle waited. The 'learner' sticker was clearly visible on the windscreen of the flashy, yellow sports car with the elaborate spoiler. He checked inside the vehicle but was puzzled to find it empty. Glancing round, he spotted an immaculately dressed and groomed, silver-haired man rummaging through a bin. A middle-aged couple who happened to be passing were horrified at the man's actions but they said nothing and just continued on their way. Patrick strolled over to the man and gently rested his arm on his shoulder.

"Come on, Larry," he said, easing a half finished sandwich out of the man's hand and letting it fall back into the bin, "I'll rustle us up somethin' decent when we get home."

Larry shrugged his shoulders and said, "Waste of good food that."

Patrick smiled sadly but kept his trap shut as he accompanied his friend back to the sports car.

Although Patrick was trying to look cool his insides were like jelly and his back was drenched in sweat. He gripped the steering wheel tightly and prepared for his next driving lesson.

"Okay, ye can start her up," Larry calmly said. Although he had seen every type of driver over the years he had never sat next to a learner in a car worth almost a quarter of a million euro.

Patrick turned on the engine and pressed down on the accelerator. The initial purr soon became an arrogant and aggressive roar as the powerful engine came alive. Larry looked at him and gave a shake of the head.

"Nice and easy just like I showed ye," he said.

Patrick caught hold of the gearstick and tried to grind it into first.

The instructor winced as he imagined the damage that his student was doing to the internal workings of the beautiful motor.

"Clutch," Larry said, making every effort to remain cool.

His student smiled and said, "Oh yeah, righ'."

The sports car bunny-hopped several times before cutting out.

"I know, I know," Patrick said. He put the car back into neutral and turned the key to the left. He tried starting the car again and the engine obediently responded, roaring into life. The gear change was much smoother this time.

"Now slowly off the clutch," Larry encouraged, "No coasting."

"Gotcha," said Patrick.

The car moved forward and off they went.

"I don't know why ye couldn't have just bought a nice little second hand motor," the older man said, "And worked yer way up from there."

"It's all about the image, Lars," Patrick said.

"What did I tell ye, I hate that bleedin' name," Larry said, chastising the learner driver. "It's Larry to you and to everyone else for that matter."

Patrick laughed, "I'm only buzzin' with ye."

The sports car approached a junction and the driver didn't appear to have any intention of stopping or at least slowing down and almost smashed into the side of a passing station wagon.

Larry jumped on his imaginary pedals while gripping the overhead handle for dear life.

"Brake, brake for Jaysus sake. This is enough to drive anyone to drink," he barked.

The sports car shuddered to a halt and Patrick glanced sideways at his ghostly looking passenger.

"Excuses, excuses," the younger man said with a grin.

Larry was unable to speak as his heart danced to its own little merry tune inside his chest. 'This was going to be one long lesson,' he thought.

After the initial rocky start things were now moving at a much smoother pace. The flash car got plenty of admiring looks soon followed by confused ones when the 'learner' stickers were spotted.

"Ah there's yer guardian angel now," Larry nonchalantly said after observing a woman waiting at the bus stop.

Patrick was too busy concentrating on his driving to notice.

"Wha'?" he said, momentarily losing his focus and grinding the gears while attempting to drop from fourth to third.

"Clutch, clutch," Larry said, chastising his student.

Patrick glanced down at the gears, struggling to find the right slot.

"If it had hair on it..." Larry said with a smirk.

"Ye dirty aul man," Patrick replied, thoroughly enjoying the banter.

"Yer guardian angel was back there," Larry said. He casually indicated with his thumb towards a bus shelter on the opposite side of the road which they had just passed.

"Are ye seein' spirits now that yer off the drink?" joked Patrick.

Larry took no notice of the jovial remark. He also loved having the craic.

"Maybe it's time we started thinkin' of puttin' ye into an aul care home or somethin'?" Patrick added with a cheeky smile.

"I'm on about the woman who rescued ye from the shop that night and put the winning lottery ticket in yer shirt pocket," the older man said.

Patrick slammed on the brakes almost giving Larry whiplash. The line of cars immediately behind was forced to take evasive action.

"Jaysus Christ. Wha' are ye up to?" said Larry, "Ye can't just stop dead."

The people in the cars agreed and let it be known with a chorus of unhappy horns.

"Don't mind them, they'll be grand," Patrick said with a wave of his hand.

Once the other drivers realised that Patrick had no intention of moving they were forced to drive round. Unsurprisingly some of them gave him the middle finger, that universal sign of disapproval. Larry slunk down in his seat while putting his hand over his face, absolutely mortified but Patrick seemed oblivious to the commotion he'd caused.

"I tell ye somethin' for nothin', there's a lot of anger in the world righ' now," he remarked.

Larry was about to respond but knew there was no point.

"You were sayin'?" Patrick said.

"I was in the back lane having a slash when I saw her struggling with ye, dragging ye out," Larry revealed. "It took her ages, the poor woman."

The younger man narrowed his eyes and said, "And why didn't ye give her a hand?"

Larry straightened himself in defence.

"I was in no fit state to help but I still felt guilty about it. Anyway, she propped ye against a wall, took a swift look round and stuffed the ticket in your pocket before disappearing again."

It was the one thing that had puzzled Patrick the most, waking up in the back lane with the winning lottery slip in his possession when he clearly remembered the shopkeeper stealing it from him. He had heard enough. He swung the steering wheel and swerved wildly across the road without checking for traffic, heading for the bus shelter.

"You'll never pass your test if ye carry on like this," Larry said, deadpan.

A motorbike Garda who was parked next to the kerb a little further along the road couldn't help but notice Patrick's reckless manoeuvre. He started up his Honda bike, gave a quick check over his shoulder and eased into traffic, cautiously following his target. Although his machine weighed almost three hundred and fifty kilos it could easily reach speeds of up to two hundred kilometres an hour if needed so he wasn't too worried about hanging back and observing proceedings from a safe distance. There was a nasty feud going on between two local drug gangs so he decided to proceed with caution just in case someone had an itchy trigger finger.

Patrick immediately recognised Janice and her two children, Jack and Emma, waiting patiently at the bus stop just ahead.

"But that's the poor woman from the graveyard I was tellin' ye about, the one who got mugged," he said in disbelief.

"Janice," Larry casually offered.

Patrick glanced at his passenger and said, "Janice, yeah. How do ye know her name?"

"She works or should I say used to work in Flynn's before you made her unemployed," said Larry.

"Wha'?" exclaimed the younger man.

"When ye killed her boss," Larry said.

"I didn't kill anyone, it was his own fault..." Patrick blurted out.

The older man smiled and said, "You need to lighten up, I was only buzzing."

"That's a very serious accusation, we don't need people hearin' things like that."

"Anyway, Janice is a lovely woman," Larry said, ignoring the driver's concerns, "She would always say hello, give me the odd cake whenever her creep of a boss wasn't looking."

"But why would she do that?" Patrick asked.

Larry gave a goofy smile. "Knows I've got a sweet tooth I suppose."

"Not the flippin' cake, the winnin' lottery ticket?" Patrick said, trying to get his head round things. "I mean she'd just lost her job..."

"Because of you," the older man pointed out but not in a malicious way.

Patrick nodded. "Yeah, righ', okay, because of me. She owes God knows how much to that lowlife moneylender fella, lives in a dump and yet she puts a lottery ticket worth millions into me pocket?"

"I guess you'll just have to ask her," Larry said with a shrug of his bony shoulders.

An almost full double-decker bus glided past the sports car on the inside lane and Janice's son, Jack, stuck his arm out at a perfect ninety degree angle to his body as if he'd been practicing for this moment all of his young life. The vehicle came to a halt. Patrick nipped into the bus lane to catch up but immediately spotted the flashing blue light from the Garda motorbike coming up behind him.

Larry also noted the lawman and said, "Best of luck talking yer way out of this one, head-the-ball."

Janice and her two children boarded the bus which resembled a formula one car it had that many sponsors plastered across it. The vehicle slowly pulled away from the kerb and continued along its journey. Patrick snatched a look at the motorbike cop in the rear view mirror and could clearly see him indicate with his gloved hand to pull over.

"Shit, we're gonna lose her," he cursed, banging the steering wheel in frustration. For a split second he contemplated speeding away but reluctantly decided to obey the law and brought the car to a halt albeit in a bunny-hop style.

Larry tilted his head and smiled at his companion.

"That's not a problem, I know where she lives," he revealed.

The usual gang of wasters and no hopers were loitering around the stairwell of the flats complex and were in no hurry to make way for Janice and her children to pass. Although she wanted to say something she held her tongue, fully aware of the consequences. She gripped Emma and Jack's small hands and dragged them along, trying to look as carefree as possible while also making sure to keep her eyes firmly fixed ahead. One of the thugs made a sexually inappropriate remark making the others laugh but Janice kept on going as if she didn't hear it. She remembered when men were real men and wouldn't have stood for this sort of behaviour but times had changed and definitely not for the better in her view. She had initially felt guilty when she'd learned from the news about the scumbag who'd mugged her, dying in Mick's bathroom. Her brain had relived the moment a thousand times. She knew that if she'd only opened the door she could have saved him. That guilt was fast evaporating however when she'd to run the gauntlet of similar scum now plaguing where she lived. How many more lives would that thug, Billy have destroyed if she'd discovered him and set him free? No, if you lived by the sword then you should be prepared to die by it too.

After negotiating the rat run below, Janice now sat on the floor of their flat next to her daughter and son, sorting through the pile of lotto slips which she'd taken from Flynn's Mini-Mart. She had ignored the plastic bag stuffed with the tickets for weeks, expecting the police to knock at the door and take her away. But that hadn't happened and the need for money to survive had grown.

"Another three plus the bonus, Ma," Emma giddily said as she held one of the tickets aloft, delighted with herself.

Janice ruffled her daughter's hair, took the slip and added it to the tidy pile of winners.

"You're a great girl, well done," she said.

The mobile phone in the minder's pocket went off. He quickly retrieved it, accepted the call and listened carefully.

"Stay there and keep watching," he ordered.

"How long will ye be?" asked the voice on the other end of the line.

"None of your fucking business," the minder coolly said. He hung up just as his boss was exiting the fancy barber shop, sporting a freshly shaven face. Frank sat into the car and looked at his driver.

"Just got a call. That Janice one has surfaced," informed the minder.

"Well what are you waitin' for?" Frank said in a menacing tone.

A loud crash startled Janice and her children as the front door was kicked in and bounced against the wall in the hall. Janice's initial thoughts were that it was the law raiding her home but she was suddenly gripped with even more fear at the thought that it could be the gang of louts from below. She nearly threw up when she saw Frank and his grinning minder appear instead. Emma and Jack instinctively grabbed onto their mother for protection and she immediately wrapped her arms around them. Frank's eyes were drawn towards the bundles of lotto slips on the floor.

He shook his head disappointedly and said, "And I always thought it was yer old man who had the gamblin' problem."

The sports car came careering around the corner with Patrick behind the wheel and Larry holding on for dear life in the passenger seat with one hand while blessing himself with the other. The brakes were pressed into action throwing the vehicle one way then another. For a chap with very little practice, Patrick was knocking it out of the park. The car came to a screeching halt almost colliding with Frank's flash motor which was going in the opposite direction. Patrick and Frank's irate minder made eye contact momentarily but the other car kept on going.

Patrick turned to Larry and said, "The head on yer man and the price of cabbage. Does he not realise that I'm almost a professional."

Larry didn't know how to respond and was just thankful that he hadn't eaten the sandwich he'd found in the cemetery bin earlier on. Patrick glanced at the welcoming party loitering at the entrance to the flats, eye-balling his smart wheels and his unconventional arrival. A long streak of misery got to his feet and Patrick copped him signalling to the others with a subtle nod of the head.

"Stay here," he told his passenger before reaching across and retrieving his imitation gun from the glove compartment.

"You're a bleeding fruit," Larry said with a shake of his head.

"This is the only language this shower of eejits understand," the younger man said. He tucked the weapon into the front of his trousers then coolly climbed out of the car making sure to keep his back to the gang. The scumbags edged closer but Patrick pretended not to notice and adjusted his suit jacket while nonchalantly rolling his neck and shoulders. When he was satisfied that he had his audience in the palm of his hand he turned round.

"Any on youse know me?" he calmly asked, staring each and every one of them in the eye.

The long streak of misery spat on the ground while another thug gave out a loud belch. Unmoved, Patrick parted his jacket and exposed his gun. There was a small but noticeable hesitancy among the gang.

"Let's keep it that way, lads," he said, "No need for anyone to die of lead poisoning today." He strolled towards the stairwell as if he owned the entire gaff. The dumbfounded scumbags parted like the Red Sea allowing him to ascend the concrete stairs unmolested.

The smashed door to Janice's flat was ajar. Patrick cautiously entered not knowing what to expect.

"Hello!" he called out, trying his best not to sound as alarmed as he felt.

There was no response so he moved further into the flat and was appalled to discover Janice sitting on the floor, cuddling her distressed children. The flat was a complete mess with broken furniture strewn all over the place. The distraught mother looked up at him. She didn't say anything at first but she didn't need to, her sad eyes said it all.

"Are ye alrigh'?" he asked even though he knew it was a stupid question and if he'd seen it happening on the television he'd be giving out.

Janice gave a slight nod of the head. Patrick wasn't sure what to do next. He spotted an action man figure on the floor, bent down and picked it up.

"Why did they do this?" he asked, referring to the men he had seen driving off minutes earlier.

"I decided that they were my redundancy, from the shop," Janice began to explain. "Not that it makes much of a difference now that Frank Harris and his goon have taken the lot."

Patrick was confused and said, "Taken wha'? You've lost me."

"The other lottery tickets. I was desperate to repay the money I borrowed from him, to get him off me back," Janice explained. "Then maybe, I don't know, things might have worked out."

Patrick manipulated the arms of the action figure, trying to get his brain around what the woman was telling him.

"But ye could have just kept the winnin' ticket and all of yer problems would have been solved in an instant," he said.

"That would have been wrong and you were so kind to us that day in the cemetery when I got..." she started to say before her voice trailed off.

Patrick shifted uneasily.

"I worked out from the letter Mick had pinned to yer chest that it was all yer idea and that ye won it fair and square," Janice said. She slowly got to her feet before wobbling a bit. Patrick quickly reached out and gently took her arm, helping to steady her. She smiled her appreciation.

"I took the security tapes from the shop, so ye wouldn't get caught," she explained, motioning towards a cushion from the couch which was discarded on the floor in the corner of the room.

Patrick picked up the cushion and undid the zip where he discovered a plastic bag containing the evidence.

"And it was a fella named Frank Harris who did this?" he asked.

"Yeah, him and his bully boy," Janice replied.

Patrick knew he had to make things right.

Detective Murphy was surrounded by several of his colleagues, studying the tape that was playing on screen in the police incident room. The footage showed Mick standing behind his shop counter talking to Billy who was clearly agitated.

"Anyone get a good look at the bloke who dropped this off?" Murphy asked.

Some of the other lawmen shook their heads while others shrugged. After Patrick had watched the tapes at home he learned that Frank Harris had been putting the squeeze on Mick for protection money. A plan of sorts began to develop, culminating with him doctoring one of the tapes, leaving enough info to implicate the gang boss. Something on screen made detective Murphy's antennae twitch.

"Rewind that bit," he excitedly told his subordinate who was holding the remote control.

The man duly obliged. Detective Murphy peered at the screen while listening intently.

"Got you, Harris," he quietly said.

The plush five-bedroom house sat detached from its neighbours in the leafy suburb just south of the capital. Cameras discreetly placed immediately below the gutters on all four corners of the building gave an almost three hundred and sixty degree view. Frank Harris had done well for himself when he'd acquired the property for half nothing more than twenty years previously. In today's market it was worth well in excess of three point five million euro. The deal involved a bag of used notes and a threat of violence against a man called Gimpy O'Donnell. Gimpy's bad luck began the day he was born and accidentally dropped, damaging his pelvis thus leading to his unfortunate moniker. And when Gimpy sided with a losing gang peddling gear in the wrong part of town he'd been left with no option other than a one way ticket to Turkey, quick smart. Frank's neighbours knew nothing of his 'business' activities and that's the way he preferred it. He'd been in the game a long time and had seen many a flash Harry meet their maker well ahead of schedule. He lived a good life but as privately as possible.

Frank narrowed his eyes as he checked the lottery slips which he'd stolen from Janice. A half-spent cigarette butt was pressed tightly between his lips and his brow was heavily wrinkled despite frequently shelling out on facials and fancy moisturisers. His minder was also working his way through the pile of tickets while sipping on a mug of tea a darker shade than mahogany. Neither man noticed the unmarked police cars rolling up outside. Detective Murphy climbed out of his vehicle relishing the thought of giving a couple of lowlifes the digs. He knew very well who Harris was but could never pin anything on him. Today was going to be a different story however. He observed his colleagues as they went through their well rehearsed routines. They were rigged out in bulletproof vests and carrying an array of armaments reminiscent of some middle-age siege. One block of a man with bulging biceps carried a sledge hammer with a head that was almost as big as a skip. Frank could imagine him back in the gym repeatedly hopping the hammer off of a truck tyre just for the fun of it. Another wiry copper with a shaven skull gripped a battering ram while several of the other officers were armed with Heckler & Koch MP7 submachine guns.

Detective Murphy curiously watched the lead Garda, an Irish boxing champion named O'Rourke who hailed from Wexford. He had never seen her fight in the flesh but had watched snippets of her in action on social media and she was very impressive to say the least. Several Gardai were also waiting at the rear of the house in case the occupants decided to do a runner which was highly likely given their unlawful occupation. As soon as everyone was in position and O'Rourke was completely satisfied, she gave the order to go.

Fragments of glass flew in all direction as Garda Thor went to war with his heavy hammer. Inside the house Frank Harris dived onto the carpeted floor and rolled towards the brick wall convinced that the place was being shot up. His minder reacted far better and pulled a telescopic baton from inside his jacket. With a flick of his wrist the weapon was extended to its full capacity.

"Open up, it's the Gardai," O'Rourke shouted.

The minder picked up a chair and flung it onto the floor just below the closest smashed window. If anyone was stupid enough to climb through there was a good chance they'd get tangled up, giving him the opportunity to strike.

"That could be anyone out there. Will we make a run for it?" Frank asked. He wasn't a coward and had no problem having a straightener with the best of them but nowadays everyone was all tooled up and not prepared to go toe to toe.

"Stay where you are, boss," the minder coolly said. He'd seen real action firsthand in the Middle East when he'd worked there doing security for a big oil company. The money had been great but there was fuck all to spend it on and there was no chance of getting the ride. When he'd convinced himself that Carl the camel had started to wink at him seductively he knew it was time to get his ass back home.

"Can you see the monitors?" Frank asked.

The minder shook his head 'no'.

"Open up, this is the Gardai," O'Rourke loudly repeated. She paused for a moment but it didn't look as if the occupants were willing to co-operate.

The reinforced front door held fast as it was repeatedly pounded by the battering ram. Although made of timber on the outside, the door was in fact constructed out of hardened steel. Frank shot his trusted minder a questioning look.

"Do you think the raid's legit?" he shouted through the din.

The minder shrugged his shoulders.

After several more unsuccessful attempts to burst through the front door O'Rourke barked an order into her radio. A split second later and the windows at the rear of the property were also put through. The minder marched over to the monitor satisfied that he wasn't going to be shot. He saw that the place was surrounded by the police.

"It's the filth alright," he said.

"What the fuck do they want?" asked Harris.

Detective Murphy stood over the gang boss and his minder who were now both lying face down on the floor with their hands cuffed firmly behind their backs. Uniformed officers were milling about in the background tearing the place apart and bagging vital evidence.

"Frank Harris, I'm arresting you in connection with the deaths of..." Garda O'Rourke began.

"Hold your fuckin' horses," shouted the gangster, trying to twist his head round to get a better look at the copper. "This is a stitch up. My brief 's going to tear you a new arsehole."

Detective Murphy moved towards Harris, accidentally standing on the scumbag's ankle.

"Argh," roared Frank Harris.

O'Rourke shot her superior a disapproving look.

"Oops," said Murphy.

Although the weather had been good of late, the evenings were now starting to get cool and the adult scholars pouring out from the community college weren't long zipping up their jackets and sticking on their trendy woollen hats. A few of them couldn't help but look on enviously at the magnificent, yellow sports car waiting in the car park before climbing into their own boring vehicles or mounting basic bicycles most likely bought second hand. Unfortunately, anything too elaborate was only asking to be robbed. The college was named after St. Jude, the patron saint of desperate cases and lost causes and was aptly named for two of its latest students. Patrick emerged from a classroom shaking his head. The discreet sign next to the door read Anger Management. Further along the corridor a similar sign indicated that the room was being used for AA meetings. Larry came out not looking best pleased. The two unlikely friends met. They stood to one side allowing the other, energetic students to pass by.

"How'd it go?" Larry asked, already guessing the answer from Patrick's demeanour.

The younger man nodded towards a quickly departing man of about forty with tinted, circular glasses.

"Grand till that specky know it all said I'd mental problems that could easily lead to violent outbursts. I could've guzzled him," he said.

"Did he really say that?" Larry asked, shocked at the lack of sensitivity.

"Not in so many words but I knew what he was thinkin'," said Patrick.

"Now, now, deep breaths," said Larry, doing his best to calm his pal.

"Wha' about yourself?" asked the younger man.

"I could murder a pint..."

Patrick raised an eyebrow.

Larry smiled and said, "...but I suppose a lemonade will have to do."

"Are ye still alrigh' to babysit tomorrow evenin'?" Patrick asked. He'd managed to get the courage up to finally ask Janice out on a date.

"Of course. Where are you taking her?"

"There's this really posh Italian restaurant in town that all the computer sites are recommendin' so I said we'd give it a go."

"Can't beat cabbage and bacon or a decent coddle," said Larry, not really gone on the fancy foreign food, "Do you even like Italian?"

"Well I'm partial to a can of spaghetti hoops, especially the alphabet ones..."

"What?"

Patrick laughed. "I'm only pullin' yer leg, ye want to see yer face," he said, "If there's nothin' I fancy I can always go for the pizza."

A 'Sale Agreed' sign was planted in the front garden of the modest, newly built house. Patrick's sports car sat idly on the brick paved driveway waiting to be pressed into action but it would be taxis all the way tonight. Him and his date were planning on having a few glasses of vino, the good stuff, with their Italian meal.

"What's seldom is wonderful," Janice had replied when she'd been asked out on the date.

Inside the house, Patrick was dressed in his smart suit with a slim fitting lilac coloured shirt and matching tie. He checked his reflection in the mirror and grinned.

"Almost perfect," he said. He made his way towards the living-room and popped his head round the door. "Are ye ready?"

Larry was lounging on the white leather couch, dressed casually in slacks and a short sleeved top like some Mafioso from the seventies. He got to his feet and picked up the large bunch of fresh white lilies off of the glass coffee table. He'd collected them only a few hours earlier from an extremely friendly and attractive florist who he reckoned was of a similar age to himself. She was a tasty bit of stuff and he noticed the absence of a wedding ring. 'With any luck she was divorced or better still, a widow, no baggage,' he thought. Another visit was definitely on the cards.

"Here," he said, thrusting the bouquet into Patrick's arms with little finesse.

"Thanks," said the younger man.

Larry smiled. "Are ye nervous?"

"Absolutely brickin' it."

"Good."

Patrick arched an eyebrow.

"It means it matters to ye," Larry said.

The two men exited the house, walked down the driveway and immediately turned left into the adjoining property which also had a 'Sale Agreed' sign hammered into the small but manicured lawn. Patrick glanced at Larry and his companion gave him a reassuring nod. Patrick rotated his neck and loosened his shoulders in an attempt to boost his confidence before pressing the bell. He couldn't help but smile when he heard the ringtone, ABBA's 'I Have A Dream' even though he'd heard it loads of times before. The door was promptly opened by Janice who was dressed to the nines. Larry gave an approving wolf whistle.

"If only I was ten years younger," he offered.

Patrick looked at his pal and pulled a face. "More like twenty with the vat at the higher rate," he said.

The older man threw Patrick an indignant look. Janice laughed at the pair of them. They really were the odd couple.

"Come in, will yis," she said, "Before the neighbours start talking."

"Ah I know them, they'll be grand," Patrick said, "Oh, here, these are for you." He awkwardly handed over the lilies having very little experience in that department.

"They're absolutely beautiful," Janice gushed, accepting the gift.

"Just like you," Patrick said, not meaning to say it aloud.

His date blushed.

Larry shook his head and muttered, "Amateur."

Larry stood in the middle of the living-room flanked by Janice's children, Jack and Emma. Janice slowly fastened the buttons on her newly purchased long black coat. She had preferred the camel coloured one that she'd tried on but reckoned she'd get more wear out of the black one especially with funerals and the like.

"Okay, all set," she said nervously. "Are ye sure you'll be all righ'?"

"I'll be grand," answered Larry.

Janice winced and said, "I was talkin' to the kids."

Patrick left out a roar of laughter which only made Janice even more embarrassed.

"Just make sure to keep him away from the bins," joked Patrick.

Jack and Emma hugged their mother and said, "We'll be fine, Ma, Larry's sound"

As Patrick and Janice stepped outside, the neighbouring door on the opposite side opened and Debbie appeared.

"Yis look only massive," she said, complimenting the pair of them.

"Howaya, Debbie," said Patrick.

Debbie checked over her shoulder and shouted, "Tommy, come out here and have a gander."

Janice was mortified but also secretly chuffed. Tommy came to the door, towelling dry his freshly washed hair.

"Ah there ye are, Patrick, Janice," he greeted. "Out on your first date then?"

Janice gave a shy smile and nodded.

"Don't get up to anythin' I wouldn't," said Tommy

Debbie immediately gave her fella a not so sly thump.

"Ouch," he said, recoiling from the playful blow. "Wha' did I say wrong?"

"And after the man buyin' us a house and you go and carryon like that," Debbie said, chastising her partner.

Patrick laughed it off. "It was the least I could do. Yis are all like me family now," he said.

His old neighbours weren't the only recipients of his generosity. When he'd purchased the three adjoining houses he'd called in to see Brian, the enthusiastic young sales assistant with the prominent Adam's apple who still worked in Kingsley Electrical. At first Brian wanted nothing to do with Patrick having been once bitten, twice shy. It was only when Patrick pulled out a huge wad of cash that the assistant realised that this was in fact the real deal. Patrick ordered and paid for a wide array of fancy appliances before giving Brian a huge tip despite the young man's protests explaining that he was going to do very well out of the commission alone. That trip to the sun for some adult fun was well and truly back on the cards.

The date between Patrick and Janice had gone surprisingly well. There hadn't been any real pauses in an otherwise naturally flowing and genuinely entertaining conversation. Janice lifted her wine glass to offer up a toast. Patrick duly obliged and raised his own. They gently clinked glasses.

"To karma," said Janice.

"And new beginnings," said Patrick.

Janice couldn't help but smile at the man opposite her. He was very different from her late husband or from any other man she'd ever known for that matter. There was a kindness in his eyes and he was very funny without even trying to be but she also felt that he was like a lost soul in need of a warm hug.

"Can I ask you a question?" she said, almost immediately regretting it.

"Fire away. I know this is all part of the interrogation process," Patrick replied before taking a cautious sip of his drink.

Janice moved uneasily in her seat. Her date raised an eyebrow in anticipation.

"Are you a gambler?" she finally asked.

"Me? No. Wouldn't know where to begin to be honest," Patrick truthfully answered. "The only thing I ever put money on was the Lotto and that's because I knew I was eventually goin' to win it."

Janice was relieved.

"Me Da had it bad though and I saw firsthand wha' it did to me poor aul Ma," he explained, thinking back to the rows when he was a child but then fondly remembering that feeling of closeness when his parents made up and he'd be sent to the far shop for choc-ices.

"Well that's good to hear," said Janice. She would tell him about her late husband's gambling problems one day but not tonight. She didn't want to spoil the occasion.

Patrick caught the attention of the lanky waiter who despite working in a restaurant looked as if he could do with a stew injection.

"Could I get the bill, please?" he politely asked.

Matchstick man duly nodded and disappeared only to return moments later with a leather bound holder containing the bill. He held it out waiting for the customers to decide which one was going to pay.

"Good man," said Patrick, accepting the holder.

The waiter nodded and was on his way again.

"He's like somethin' out of Belson," Patrick said but not in a mean way.

"He's very thin all righ'," Janice agreed. "Could have an eating disorder, the poor chap."

"I thought that was only a woman's thing," Patrick said.

Janice shook her head sadly. "Not at all. I was only watchin' one of them chat shows recently and they were sayin' that there's been a huge increase in men sufferin' from body image issues."

"Jaysus, ye live and learn. I'm lucky to go an hour or two without grub before gettin' hangry," Patrick said, "And I never seem to put on weight."

Janice laughed and said, "Maybe ye've a tape worm?"

Patrick gave a contemplative look.

"Maybe yer righ', I'll have to take a look when I get home," he replied, deadpan.

Janice scrunched her face at the thought and was expecting her date to laugh but he didn't. He was too busy throwing his eye over the itemised bill as if he was checking that everything was above board but in reality he couldn't give a toss. Tonight had been fantastic and he couldn't have put a price on it. He stuck his hand into his trouser pocket and searched around but came up short. He then patted his shirt pocket before checking his jacket.

Janice leaned forward. "Is everythin' all right?" she asked in a hushed voice.

Patrick looked at his date and pulled a face.

"We migh' have to do a runner, I can't find me bleedin' wallet," he whispered back.

"You're not serious?" said Janice, her face whitening despite a liberal application of make-up.

Patrick nodded.

She began to root through her handbag. "I might have some cash," she said, staring into her bag, She always paid her own way but Patrick had been insistent that tonight was on him, "How much is it for?" she asked.

Patrick glanced down at the bill and said, "Two hundred and thirty-two euro without the tip."

Janice lifted her head and looked at her date. "Sweet Mother of God, how much?" she said, nearly choking.

"I know, its extortion. Think I migh' have to invest in a place like this for meself," Patrick nonchalantly replied.

While Janice was frantically going through her handbag Patrick was casually looking out through the huge expanse of glass and onto the main road. A vaguely familiar car with steam billowing from the pores of the bonnet slowly rolled into view. A man was walking alongside the vehicle while leaning in through the open driver's window and steering it. It took a few seconds for Patrick to register that the bloke was none other than medallion man himself, Simon. At the rear of the vehicle using all of her ample mass was a dishevelled looking Mandy. Patrick immediately jumped to his feet and raced over to the glass. He clenched his fist and was about to bang on the window when he had a sudden change of heart. He eased open his hand and let it drop slowly to his side. Janice was oblivious to Patrick's shenanigans as she desperately rummaged deeper into her handbag.

"What's this..." she said to herself.

Out on the street, Mandy had decided to take a short break to catch her breath leaving Simon with no other choice but to wait. She happened to glance over in Patrick's direction, not recognising him at first. He could see the confusion on her face when it eventually registered with her who he was. She continued to stare, not believing that her ex could afford to dine in such a fancy restaurant. Patrick gave a slight sort of apologetic nod before returning to his seat where Janice was now examining a brand new bank card which she'd removed from an envelope. Out of the corner of his eye Patrick noticed Mandy and Simon resuming their pushing duties and within a few short moments they were gone again.

"I don't own a credit card, never have," Janice said, confused. She narrowed her eyes and looked suspiciously at her date but he just smiled, giving nothing away.

"Who's name is on it?" he asked.

"Mine," answered Janice.

"Sure give it to the waiter and see what happens," Patrick said, "And if it doesn't work you migh' want to take off those fancy heels and get ready to leggit."

The couple stood next to an ATM machine only a short distance from the posh restaurant where Janice's mystery credit card had worked perfectly. She double-checked the

PIN number written on the envelope before pressing enter on the keypad. The machine accepted the code and a list of options were then presented. She looked at Patrick and he gave her an encouraging nod. She pressed the balance option and nearly fainted when the amount displayed showed nine hundred and ninety-nine thousand, seven hundred and fifty euro.

"The two hundred and fifty euro including tip from the restaurant would have made it an even million," Patrick calmly explained.

"But I don't understand," Janice barely managed to say, "You've already bought me and the kids a brand new house?"

"If you hadn't given me back the winnin' ticket I'd have had nothin'," he said.

Janice shook her head. "It was yours, fair and square."

"It's too much money for any one person to have," he said, "And besides..." He looked away, embarrassed.

Janice felt as if she was caught up in some sort of a dream and waited to be booted up the arse and back to reality.

Patrick pursed his lips giving him a moment to gather himself. "I figured that if you'd enough money and didn't need anythin' else from me..."

"Would I still be interested?" she interjected.

"Yep."

"You can't buy love," she said.

Janice threw her arms around Patrick's neck and pulled him closer. They kissed clumsily at first before getting a better handle on things and after a few moments everything felt so natural. They eventually broke free after almost running out of oxygen and stood there gazing into one another's eyes like a pair of besotted teenagers.

"I love you," Janice softly said.

Finally, after years of aimlessly existing Patrick finally felt complete.

"I love you too," he said, then went in for another marathon snog.

****

About the Author

Patrick was born in Lower Gardiner Street in 1971 in the heart of Dublin's north inner-city and attended St. Paul's CBS, North Brunswick Street. In 1992 he qualified as an Amenity Horticulturist from the National Botanic Gardens in Glasnevin and has worked in some of the most prestigious gardens in Ireland including Áras an Uachtaráin. He now resides in County Kerry with his wife, Liz. Baxter's Boys, Patrick's debut novel was published in 2020 to rave reviews and is available to borrow from over forty libraries across Ireland. A former member of Filmbase, Patrick is currently working on a feature length screenplay called 'No Time For Cowboys', a harrowing tale of marital break-up and the devastating consequences for all involved. He has written and directed a number of short plays including Sam Who?, Bar Flies, A Fishy Tale & Bin Wars! In 2022 Patrick was one of nine writers selected by The Irish Writers' Centre in Dublin for their Duo Membership/Mentorship Programme. He has been a guest speaker at a number of events including the Liverpool Writing OnThe Wall Festival and the Dingle Literary Festival.

Baxter's Boys Reviews

"Packed with Dublin slang, it will appeal to fans of Roddy Doyle's Barrytown Trilogy and will resonate far beyond the rutted Sunday league football pitches." – Irish Independent.

"The Snapper meets Fever Pitch with a dose of Shameless thrown in for good measure." – Dublin's Northside People.

"If you liked the spirit of the movie The Full Monty, then you'll love this book." – Meath Chronicle.

"Someone needs to call Netflix. This has series written all over it." – Goodreads review.

"Although the cover would suggest that this is a football story, there is so much more to it than that... Simply put, it has all the ingredients to make it to the screen." Amazon review.

Please Review

If you enjoyed this book, I would really appreciate if you could leave a review on Amazon or Goodreads. Your opinion counts and it does influence buyer decision on whether to purchase the book or not. Thank You!